March's Luck

A Larry Macklin Mystery-Book 5

A. E. Howe

Books in the Larry Macklin Mystery Series:

November's Past (Book 1)

December's Secrets (Book 2)

January's Betrayal (Book 3)

February's Regrets (Book 4)

March's Luck (Book 5)

April's Desires (Book 6)

May's Danger (Book 7)

ISBN: 0-9862733-4-1
ISBN-13: 978-0-9862733-4-6

DEDICATION

For Mom

CHAPTER ONE

I walked into the sheriff's office on a Tuesday morning and waved to Dill Kirby, the semi-retired sergeant working the front desk. He gave me a broad smile.

"Mornin', Larry! She beat ya in," he said loudly and laughed wickedly at my expense.

"Thanks, old man," I threw back at him, but he just shook his head and chuckled.

I walked down the hall and turned the corner into the large open area that housed the criminal investigations department. Adams County is small and rural, so there were only ten desks in the room. Mine sat between the desk of my old partner, Pete Henley, and that of my new partner, Darlene Marks. Darlene was at her desk, staring at her monitor. A big mug of coffee from the Fast Mart sat by her elbow, while her leg tapped quickly up and down.

I tried to be inconspicuous as I walked over to my desk. All I wanted was a couple of minutes to sit down and look over any reports that had been assigned to me from the night before and to generally wake up. I knew that I didn't stand a chance.

"Morning, rookie!" Darlene said cheerfully. Way too cheerfully for eight-thirty in the morning.

"Why do you call me that? I've been working here for nearly seven years. You're the one that started barely a week ago," I grumbled at her. We'd been over this ground before.

"I've been in law enforcement for ten years, pal. Your dad's just got you showing me around. It's not like you're my field training officer."

"You're not my FTO either, so stop calling me rookie," I said.

"You have got to learn to take a joke. Everyone should have a nickname. Like your old partner, Deputy Barf," she said lightly.

I looked longingly over at Pete's desk. He was probably eating breakfast at the Donut Hole right now. He had never come in and called me names before nine o'clock in the morning. I missed working with Pete a lot.

"We've got some doozies from last night," Darlene went on. "Here's one we can work on together," she said, handing me a copy of a report from patrol.

Lt. Johnson came in around seven every morning and went through the previous night's reports and assigned them to investigators. Easy cases could be handled by one investigator, but for something more serious we'd team up with our partners and work them together. Since Darlene had become my partner, I'd found that I was willing to work on some pretty big cases by myself. But if she asked for my help on a case, I really couldn't refuse.

"Somebody stole a backhoe. Brand new. Thing's worth twenty-five thousand."

"That's less than some cars," I said, not wanting to be drawn into it.

"Yeah, but they almost ran over some homeless guy on their way out of the yard with it. Knocked him down. Could have killed him." Darlene got excited easily. Though, looking over the report, I had to admit that we could bring some pretty serious charges against the thief.

The homeless man had been taken to a hospital in Tallahassee. "Contacting the hospital would be one of the first steps," I said reluctantly. Glancing over at Darlene, I saw that she was already on the phone. She mouthed: *Calling the hospital.* I sighed and went back to looking over my own assignments.

An hour later we pulled into the parking lot of Mill's Lumber and Supply. They were the local John Deere dealership and it was their backhoe that had gone missing.

The manager, Dave Rudd, took us out back.

"Damned thing. I got a call from the alarm company about two o'clock. Now, that ain't unusual, stupid thing goes off a couple times a month. Can't get them to fix it right. Anyway, that's why I wasn't too excited. I got dressed, with my wife cussin' up a storm about being woke up again, and headed out to my truck. That's when I got a call from one of your deputies that the fence was all tore to hell and some guy was hurt. Well, I didn't know who he was talking about. We don't have a night watchman or anything. Of course, now that I think about it, a night watchman might not be a bad idea."

Dave kept talking all the way to the back lot. I listened with half an ear while Darlene took meticulous notes. Not easy since she was walking too.

"He cut our chain, then backed up and hooked his truck up to the trailer. Guess we shouldn't have left it on the trailer, but who the hell would think someone would cut through the lock?" Dave said, shaking his head.

We looked at the chain and lock. The chain was heavy-duty, but the lock, not so much. The thief had cut the lock off and was in like Flynn.

"I'll be glad to come out and give your place a security check," Darlene told Dave. They wandered off, talking about all the problems of securing a large site, while I looked around the grounds. Attached to the report was a picture of the backhoe and trailer that were stolen. From where I stood, I could see at least three pieces of heavy equipment that looked more expensive and just as easy to steal.

"Why do you think they took that backhoe?" I asked

Rudd. He stopped and looked at me, slightly puzzled.

"You know, I wondered that myself."

"The report said they also broke into your office. Where is that?" Darlene asked him.

"Over here," he said, leading us to a small annex built onto the store with a sign over the door that read "John Deere Sales". He pointed to the door, which looked like someone had just taken a crowbar and levered the door open. Sykes, the deputy responding, had dusted the door and the office for prints. With small cases, our deputies often do the evidence collection themselves.

"They took the keys. In fact, they took a lot of keys," Dave said, sounding a bit tired. "I'm going to have to get replacement keys for all of the equipment they didn't steal." A thought occurred to him. "You don't think they're planning on coming back for the other rigs, do you?"

"No. I'm sure they took all the keys 'cause they didn't know which set went to the one they were going to steal," I reassured him.

"The good news is that probably means it's not an inside job," Darlene said, making notes. *Points to her*, I thought.

"Ohhhh, I see. Because if it was one of our guys, he'd know which set of keys went with which backhoe. Yeah, gee, I hadn't even thought it could have been one of our employees. Wow, that *is* good news."

"Interesting," Darlene said. She had an irritating habit of making you ask what she was talking about, but this time I was on top of it.

"You're right," I told her. "The thief didn't ransack the office."

Dave looked back and forth between Darlene and me. I explained, "That means our bad guy wasn't after money. Which was also my point about the backhoe he stole. It wasn't the most valuable one on your lot."

Dave nodded thoughtfully.

"Gooseneck trailer, right?" I asked.

"Yep, you don't want something that big and heavy

hanging off your bumper," he said, falling quickly into the cadence of a sales pitch.

I held up my hand and called dispatch, asking if they had any reports of a truck being stolen in the last forty-eight hours.

"Bingo," I said after getting contact info from the dispatcher. "A dually was stolen from a farm south of town last night."

"The plot thickens," Darlene said with way too much enthusiasm.

Before we left I turned to Dave. "This may be a stupid question, but what would someone do with that particular piece of equipment?"

"Dig a hole, fill in a hole, or both," he answered, eyebrows raised. I nodded. *Stupid question.*

After we'd been out and talked with the farmer whose truck was stolen, I was forced to admit to myself—not to Darlene, but just to myself—that this case was a lot more interesting than I'd thought it would be when I read the report.

"The thief had to know where that truck was," Darlene said as I drove. We'd decided to go to the Donut Hole for lunch. With Winston's Grill closed after the owner had turned out to be a homicidal maniac, the Donut Hole had ramped up their lunch menu, adding wraps and more sandwiches.

"Yep," I agreed. The farm was pretty far out of town. "Which means that's probably our best chance. There has to be a connection. Our crook could be a family member, friend, neighbor or an ex-employee."

"Or possibly he spotted the truck in town and decided that was the one he wanted, then followed the truck out to the farm."

"Maybe, but he'd be taking a chance. How would he know that the owner left the keys in the truck?" I asked. Though, honestly, that wasn't as rare on a farm as it would be in town. A farmer could have several farmhands that might need to use the truck, so sometimes it was just easier to leave the keys in the vehicle so that anyone that needed it didn't have to hunt up the person with the keys.

We took our sandwiches and sat at one of the picnic tables outside the small restaurant. With Darlene eating and not talking, I enjoyed my lunch and the quiet, watching a steady stream of folks come and go. The loss of Winston's had been a godsend for the Donut Hole.

The weather was perfect. The sun was shining in a clear blue sky and a cool breeze blew through the trees. In north Florida the worst of the winter weather is usually over by mid-March. There can still be the occasional freeze or days of rain, but most days are like this, making you want to spend them lying in the grass and staring up at the sky.

The peace of the afternoon was shattered when I heard the screech of brakes. I looked up to see a small, bright red car make a sharp turn into the parking lot. The driver was short and something about the profile set the hairs on the back of my neck on end. The car slammed to a stop and the door was open before the vehicle had stopped rocking back and forth.

"Damn it!" I blurted out involuntarily, looking for some way to escape. Darlene just stared at the wild-eyed, black-haired woman who came stomping over to our table.

"You haven't answered any of my texts," Marcy Pike loudly accused me.

I stood up, facing my ex-girlfriend. "Just calm down. I don't have to answer your texts," I said reasonably. "Besides, I haven't gotten most of them because I blocked you after I got the first one."

Her face turned a dangerous, fiery red. "You son of a—" Surprisingly, she stopped herself. "Look, I just want to talk to you." Marcy had turned the volume on her voice down by half, trying to sound sane.

I looked around at the dozen people, including Darlene, who'd stopped eating in order to watch the show. "Fair enough," I said, turning back to her. "Let's go over to your car."

One of the things that galled Marcy the most was someone being rational, but she seemed to swallow her desire for battle and nodded.

I took out my phone as we walked to her car. "Let me finish this text," I said when we stopped. On my phone I typed out: *watch us. if things get ugly come break it up*, and sent the text to Darlene.

"Are you done?" Marcy asked with narrowed eyes as I put my phone away.

"Sorry," I said, trying to throw some water on whatever fire she wanted to get started. "I heard your dad's been sick. I hope he gets better soon."

"He's pretty bad off. He's in hospice now," Marcy said and, for a moment, there was real emotion in her voice. But it was all gone by the time she spat out the next sentence. "Look, I need any of my stuff that you still have."

"What stuff? We lived together, like, nine years ago," I reminded her.

"I know I left some stuff when I moved out," Marcy said accusingly.

"Maybe. I don't know. Some junk, yeah. But I've moved twice since then." The first time I'd moved after she left me was because I was afraid she'd come back, but I decided pointing that out wouldn't help the situation.

"Are you telling me you threw it out?" It was like watching a locomotive start moving down the track. I could see the pressure building up behind her eyes.

"Yes. I don't think there was anything but some old makeup, maybe some towels, an old pair of sandals. Literally just junk," I told her, trying to think of anything else she might have left and what she could possibly want with it now.

"That was my stuff," she said, glaring at me.

"Well, maybe you should have gotten it when you moved out," I answered, exasperated.

I watched as she calculated how far to take this. Suddenly, her eyes shifted. "Yeah, okay. You're saying you don't have anything of mine?"

"That's right." I knew that she'd shifted into plotting mode. Not a good sign, but I couldn't do anything about it.

"Fine, be that way." Marcy threw open the door to her car, trying to hit me with it, and dropped into the driver's seat. I moved away quickly, knowing that if she had the opportunity she'd run me over as she left the parking lot. From a safe distance, I watched her spin out of the driveway.

A boxy sedan that I recognized pulled in seconds after Marcy took off down the road. "Was that who I think it was?" Pete asked me after he got out.

"I don't want to talk about it," I said good-naturedly.

"I understand that, brother." Pete and I hadn't known each other back when I was dating Marcy, but he'd heard the stories, both from me and from mutual friends. He looked over at the Donut Hole. "I sure miss Winston's." He held up his hand to stop me. "Not Winston himself. That guy can rot in hell."

"How's Mary doing?" I asked.

"Confused. Trying to understand everything." Pete shrugged. "It has to be tough when you find out your loving father is a serial killer."

"You ready to go, rookie?" Darlene asked, coming up behind me.

I rolled my eyes so that only Pete could see. "Talk to you later," I told him, longing for the days when we were partners.

I'd just pulled the car out of the driveway when the dispatch radio cut in to tell us that Sergeant Will Toomey was requesting our presence out at Parrish Farm, but not giving any details. Whenever possible, our dispatchers tried to be discreet. Even in this day and age of two hundred TV channels and the Internet, a few folks in the county still had police band scanners. And they also had cell phones; if they heard something really exciting going down on the radio, they'd text it to half the county.

If Toomey wanted us, then it was important. Once I was headed that way, I called him on my phone.

"Possibly an accident, but equally likely it's a homicide. And no one is going to be happy about the victim," Toomey said sadly. "It's Mr. Parrish himself."

Damn it, I thought. Hank Parrish was one of the richest farmers in the county and a model human being. More personally, he'd been a great friend to my dad, helping him with his first election to sheriff and supporting him ever since.

Parrish land covered thousands of acres spread over a large part of the county. Toomey gave me directions to a hay field a quarter mile from the main house. I told him we'd be there in fifteen minutes and hung up.

CHAPTER TWO

Toomey met us at the gate to the hay field. A white truck sat just inside the gate. A middle-aged Hispanic man was standing next to the open door, looking very upset.

"Joe Parrish told our friend here to ride out and see if he could find Hank Senior. He found him lying in the field and called 911."

"Did he call Joe?" I asked. Toomey shrugged. Darlene and I walked over to the man.

"What's your name?"

"Carlos Ruiz. Please, I got to call Mr. Joe."

"You called 911?"

"I see a body. I call the police, then the woman on the phone says to wait and not call anyone else. I told her I had to call Mr. Joe, it was his father who was dead, but she said no. Go to the gate and wait for the deputy. So I did, but now you're here. I got to call. It's his father." The man seemed to be in genuine shock.

"Better leave your car here. I can't tell if we have tire tracks or not," Toomey said somberly. "I walked on the left side of these ruts."

I told Carlos to wait for us and we fell in line behind Toomey, heading out into the pasture.

I looked at the field. It was two hundred acres, bordered by old growth hardwoods. Looking ahead, I couldn't see any vehicles or buildings. I knew that the Parrish family had owned the land for well over a hundred years. This case was going to be a bear to deal with no matter how you looked at it. The victim was a very important and well-liked member of the community, so all the stresses of a murder investigation would be multiplied a dozen times.

"It's not too much farther," Toomey said over his shoulder as he traipsed alongside the dual ruts that bordered the edge of the hay field. He set a steady pace. Middle-aged, he also served in the Army Reserve. Of average height and build, his eyes had a military squint that told anyone with two brain cells that this was not a person who played games and that, if you chose to play games with him, he was going to win.

As we got closer to the murder site, I saw an area where the open pasture cut into the woods. Off to the right I could see a large tractor parked at an odd angle and, in the distance, the railroad tracks that ran along the far edge of the pasture.

"It ain't pretty," Toomey warned. "I'm going to go back and wait for Shantel and Marcus," he said, referring to our best crime scene techs.

As irritating as I found Darlene, I knew that she was highly competent and would follow in my footsteps as we tried to avoid tramping over any evidence that might exist on the soft soil surrounding the body.

I winced when I saw Hank Parrish lying on the ground about twenty feet from the tractor. He was on his back, an arrow sticking out of his left eye. I understood Toomey's uncertainty about whether this was a murder or an accident. Every year we dealt with several hunting accidents. Usually they were just gunshot wounds, but occasionally it was something more exotic. Last year a young man got his foot tangled up in his deer stand and fell headfirst onto the ground from fifteen feet up, breaking his neck. On average, every other hunting season someone out in the woods ended up dead.

"Couldn't have been hunting deer. Season's been over for months," Darlene said, peering around me and trying to get a closer look.

I looked in the direction that the arrow had probably traveled. "Still legal to hunt boar or small game."

"You got to get close for those. They'd have been able to see him. Hell, he's wearing a red shirt," Darlene pointed out.

"You've got to get pretty close anytime you're using a bow."

"That's true."

"We'll have to wait till they photograph and document the scene before we can get a closer look, but I'm inclined to agree with you that an accident seems pretty unlikely."

I pulled out my phone and called Dad. He was in Tallahassee at a regional law enforcement meeting, but said that he would come by the crime scene when the meeting was over. He'd already heard about the death. I could hear the weariness in his tone.

"Let's go find the family and let them know," I told Darlene. "We won't be able to keep a lid on it much longer."

We went back up to the gate where Toomey was having a hard time keeping a handle on Carlos.

"He's getting himself all worked up," Toomey told me.

"We're going to tell the family now."

No sooner had the words left my mouth than a truck came down the road, moving fast, and pulled onto the side of the road behind the other vehicles. A large, stocky man I recognized as Joe Parrish, in his late forties and the eldest of the Parrish children, jumped down from the cab and strode over to us.

"What's going on?" He saw Carlos. "Where's my father?"

I stepped up to him. "I'm Deputy Larry Macklin with the sheriff's office."

He turned and focused his attention on me. "You're the sheriff's son."

"That's right. Mr. Parrish, I think you'd better prepare yourself." I paused to give my words time to sink in.

His face took on a puzzled expression, as though the thought of bad news was alien to him. "Why? What's happened?"

"I'm afraid that your father is dead." I didn't want to tell him that he'd been murdered yet. Who knew? Maybe he'd blurt out something like: *Who shot my father with an arrow?* and I could arrest him on the spot.

He fell back against the hood of Toomey's patrol car. "He was fine this morning. Dad was just at the doctor's a month ago." Joe spoke slowly, his eyes focused on the ground. "I… What?" He tried to puzzle it through. "Was it an accident? Like I said, he was feeling fine."

"For the moment, we can't be sure what killed him," I said, thinking: *The arrow sticking through his skull is a big clue, though.* My dark humor almost caused me to laugh out loud. My dad and I had the occasional odd tendency to laugh at funerals and other situations surrounding death. It was either a coping mechanism, or we were just weird. "I *can* tell you that it looks like it was quick. The coroner's office will be here soon, and we will be working very hard to get some answers for you. We're going to want to talk with your family and employees."

"Sure," Joe said, clearly stunned by the news. I knew what it was like to have a father who was bigger than life. Losing Hank Parrish would leave a huge void that would take a long time to fill.

"What do you suspect?" Joe asked suddenly. He was smart—I knew that from his reputation. I had also heard he was a cutthroat businessman. Not that I blamed him. It was hard to make a living as a farmer.

"I'd be a poor investigator if I suspected anything at this point. It's very early days. What we have to do is gather as much information as we can. Anyone who has been on this property in the past twenty-four hours, or could have been on the property, needs to be questioned. I know that this will be a difficult time. Unfortunately, we're going to have to make it even worse by conducting an investigation while you and your family are still grieving."

He stared at me hard. "When do you want to talk to the family?"

I looked at Darlene, standing by me quietly and respectfully. I decided that it would be best if both of us did the questioning. "Give us a couple of hours."

"I can get the employees together at any time," Joe said with authority. The king was dead, long live the king.

"We'll talk to them after we've talked with the family. What you can do now is make a list of all the employees that are here today, and make sure they don't leave until we've spoken with them."

He nodded, then Darlene and I headed back to the crime scene.

I wanted to walk around looking for evidence, but I needed to wait for the techs to do their thing. Shantel Williams and Marcus Brown were the best we had, and I knew they would try to find every spot of blood and stray piece of trash at the scene and flag and photograph it before bagging and logging it in. I had to keep reminding myself that patience and due diligence were my friends.

I could tell that Darlene was itching to get started too. I was willing to admit that on the few cases we'd worked together so far, I had been impressed with her obsessive need to figure everything out. This was both a blessing and a curse. Even on the tightest cases I'd put together, there were always unanswered questions. At some point during an investigation you just had to accept that you knew everything you were going to know and let it go on up the food chain to the prosecutor's office.

"The arrow probably came from that direction." Darlene pointed off into the dense woods where Parrish must have been looking when he was struck by the arrow.

"That's a good bet."

Darlene turned to Shantel, who was walking around putting flags in the ground near possible evidence. "Can we borrow the video camera?" Darlene asked her.

Shantel picked up the camera and walked over to Darlene. "Have you got him trained yet?" she asked as I felt my face flush.

"Getting there. The good news is, I think he *is* trainable," Darlene told her.

I felt like they were in a secret club where the sole purpose was to get under my skin. Maybe this was a little taste of what women felt like when there were only men around. I looked to Marcus for support, but he was pretending not to hear.

"Be nice. I owe him," Shantel said, looking over at me with a smile that made my irritation meter go back down to green. Through a bit of good luck, and with the help of two other deputies, I'd managed to find and rescue her missing niece the month before. Ever since, the tough-talking Shantel had been sickeningly grateful to me. I thought about telling her, for the hundredth time, that I'd been lucky and that she owed Pete and Deputy Julio Ortiz as much as me, but there wasn't any point.

"Come on. I'll film, you keep your eye out for any evidence," Darlene told me.

As frustrating as it was to admit to myself, Darlene was smart to grab the camera. We could have used one of our cell phones, but the quality was better on the crime scene camera and the time was calibrated and would be in sync with all the other footage of the crime scene.

We hadn't gone more than ten feet past the dense oak scrub and wax myrtle at the edge of the woods before the area opened up a bit and made it easier to walk. There was a clearing with half a dozen large live oak trees about fifty feet inside of the woods. Along the far edge of the clearing, I could see the railroad embankment a hundred and fifty feet away.

"Damn!" Darlene exclaimed when she stepped into the clearing. She had the camera focused on the ground ahead of us. There were a dozen freshly dug holes scattered randomly throughout the clearing. "What the hell happened here?"

I was too busy examining the holes to answer her. They varied in size from some that were big enough to bury a microwave to several that you could have dropped a refrigerator into. Near the holes were the remains of an old house, its ancient brick chimney still standing tall. The railroad tracks were just beyond the house.

"These were dug very recently," Darlene said, as much to herself as to me. We walked carefully around the area.

"What do you think they were doing?"

"It might have nothing to do with the murder. Could be something the Parrishes were working on." I didn't want to start focusing on the holes as clues until we knew more.

"Look." Darlene pointed with the camera toward large tire tracks in the dirt. The tracks went off down a dirt path, large enough for a car or tractor, but clearly seldom used.

"Let's follow them," I said. Darlene was already on the trail, which sloped down through some thick undergrowth.

"Son of a…" Darlene breathed. She stopped short and I almost bumped into her. I'm sure my mouth fell open. In another small clearing was the trailer and backhoe that had been stolen. The backhoe was leaning half off of the trailer.

"That's Turner Road," Darlene said, aiming the camera fifty feet on the other side of the trailer and backhoe.

"Looks like they tried to get it back on the trailer and missed the ramp," I said.

"The way it's resting there, I bet it's stuck."

I could see that the backhoe's transfer case was jammed into the ramp.

"So someone stole the backhoe to come out here and dig holes. Why?" I asked.

"And is it connected to our murder?" Darlene threw in.

"Seems likely. I can accept some coincidences, but this would be a stretch." Then a thought occurred to me. "Maybe they planned on burying the body."

"I like that theory," Darlene said. "Which would mean that it was premeditated."

"They stole the backhoe last night and came out here to dig a hole in order to bury the body of a man they hadn't killed yet. They killed Parrish this morning and then… What? They got spooked?"

"If that was the plan, then they'd have to know that Parrish was going to be out here, or have some way of getting him out here."

"It's a bit far fetched, but it explains the backhoe and the holes."

"Wait. Then why dig a dozen holes?"

I looked at the backhoe sitting precariously tilted off the ramp. "A backhoe isn't quite as easy to operate as a car. I'd say whoever stole this didn't have much experience. Maybe some of the holes were for practice. Or maybe they wanted it to look like the whole area was dug up, so there wouldn't be just one freshly turned, grave-like patch of ground." Darlene shrugged, which summed up how happy I was with my own theory. "Call someone to come around on Turner Road with some crime scene tape," I said.

Darlene took out her radio and got patched through to a deputy who was at the entrance to the pasture. After telling him what she needed, she added, "And don't be stupid and pull onto the dirt road. We need to cast any tire tracks that are there."

I heard, "Yeah, yeah, I'm not a moron," come over the radio.

"Of course, the tires probably belong to the truck that was stolen," I said, but we both knew that an investigation could be botched by making assumptions.

Ten minutes later we had the road taped off and we headed back to the spot where Parrish had been killed. Shantel and Marcus were carefully lifting tire casts from tracks on the ground near the body, even though Toomey figured they probably belonged to Mr. Ruiz. We told them that they had some additional tire tracks to cast in the woods.

"Don't feel compelled to find us more work," Shantel joked.

Two forensic techs who worked for our coroner, Dr. Darzi, had finished photographing the body and were in the process of bagging the hands and carefully examining clothes, mouth, nostrils and hair.

They used a vacuum to pick up any fibers, hairs and minerals on the outside of his clothes before turning him over onto a body bag. The procedure was made more awkward than usual because they had to keep from moving the crossbow bolt sticking out of his eye. As they turned the body, I had a chance to see that the bolt hadn't gone all the way through the skull.

"Depending on the pull weight of the crossbow, I'd guess that the killer wasn't too far from the victim," Darlene said from behind me.

"I'll get Darzi to check with his fellow forensic pathologists and come up with a chart that shows estimated distance, pull weight and penetration. He'll love it."

"After you've looked at a hundred automobile accidents, it might be easy to get excited about something exotic like a crossbow killing."

"Have you worked with him before?" I asked. Darlene had been with the Calhoun Police Department most of her career, but it was a small force and the sheriff's department wound up doing most of the serious crime investigations for both the city and county.

"Only on auto accidents. Though the Danfield accident *did* turn into vehicular homicide. I worked with him and the State Attorney on that case," she said.

I didn't remember the case, but I didn't ask any questions. Once Darlene got going on a story, you couldn't get a word in until she'd given you every detail.

I heard a vehicle approaching and turned to see Dad's truck driving toward us, a "Re-Elect Sheriff Ted Macklin" sign displayed prominently on the driver's door. He parked twenty yards away and got out of the truck, still in the full uniform he'd worn to the regional meeting. Normally, he wore what he called his "small town sheriff's uniform"— jeans, a button-down shirt with his badge on it, cowboy boots and his stainless steel 1911 close at hand in a tooled leather holster. But today he cut an imposing figure as he walked across the field, his badge and the brass stars on his lapel flashing in the sun.

"Sad," he said when he got up beside me. He stepped closer to examine the head wound as Darzi's team tried to figure out how to zip up the body bag around the bolt.

Finally one of them said, "Duct tape. And bring another body bag. We'll cut it up and use that to wrap the head."

Once they'd protected the head as much as they were able, they put the body in their van and drove off. I hadn't bothered to ask them any questions because everything would be contingent on the results of the full autopsy. Lately Dr. Darzi had cracked down on his teams speculating about the time or cause of death while at the scene.

I filled Dad in on the backhoe and what we had found in the woods.

"We're ready to go up to the house and talk to the family. While we're gone I'll have Toomey get a couple of other deputies to help Marcus and Shantel search the area for additional evidence."

"You mind if I follow you all up there and pay my respects to the family?" Dad asked me, looking over at Darlene so as to include her in the request. Even though he was the boss, he always tried to defer to his investigative teams on an active case.

"I don't think that can hurt," I said.

"Might even help. They'll feel like you're showing them the respect they deserve. Being big fish," Darlene said, and I had to agree. If they knew right from the start that the big guy was overseeing the investigation, they'd be less likely to start demanding to speak to our supervisor.

I called Joe Parrish and told him we were headed up to the house.

"I've got most of the family here," he said over the muffled sound of crying in the background.

CHAPTER THREE

As soon as we got in the car Darlene said, "Hank Junior. I'd like to know where he was."

"You know him?" I asked.

"Is there a law enforcement officer within two hundred miles that doesn't?" she asked and I saw her point. "I had a couple run-ins with him, mostly drunk and disorderly. But once he wrote a bad check at the bank. Forged it, actually. We had him dead to rights, but his dad changed his mind at the last minute and refused to press charges. Said he'd forgotten that he'd given Junior permission to sign his name. Of course, everyone at First City Bank was more than happy to go along with anything Mr. Parrish said."

"When you're an addict, you act like an addict. It doesn't matter whose son you are or how you were raised. But why would he steal a backhoe? And I'd bet even he knows how to use one. That's where the backhoe is going to bite us in the butt. Everyone on the farm probably knows how to use a backhoe, and I bet they own at least two or three."

"True," she responded.

We pulled up to the house—a large, white, two-story clapboard structure with a wide front porch. Over one hundred years old, the house looked more utilitarian than ostentatious. Two cars and three trucks were parked in the driveway.

We let Dad take the lead. He was met by Joe, who came out on the porch to greet us.

"My sisters are pretty upset," he said as he ushered us into the hallway that stretched the full length of the house. We could hear sobbing as soon as we entered. We followed Joe into a large living room on the right-hand side of the hallway.

Joe's two sisters were sitting on a sofa, wiping their eyes as we came in. Three men stood in various poses around the room, looking uncomfortable.

"My sisters, Jane and Marge," Joe said, beginning the introductions. Jane was in her mid-to-late thirties, attractive and professionally dressed. Her older sister Marge had too much jaw and her hair was in a messy bun. Marge's clothes spoke more of the farm than the office.

"Marge's husband, Clive," Joe continued, pointing to a man wearing jeans and a dirty polo. "And Jane's friend, Andrew Simmons." Andrew looked like a lawyer, which I was soon to find out was his profession.

"And my brother, Hank," Joe finished, pointing to a downcast man in his early thirties standing in a corner of the room. I was struck by how much Hank Junior looked like his father. And since he hadn't always taken care of himself, he didn't even look that much younger than his father. Hard drinking and rough living can do that to you.

"I hope I don't have to tell you that we're going to take this case seriously... and personally. Your father was a very good friend to me. I don't think I would have been elected sheriff without his support. But we need something from all of you." Dad paused for dramatic effect. "We're going to have to spend some time asking you all some very personal questions about your family. I couldn't feel worse about this, but there's no other way for us to get this investigation off on the right start."

He stopped a moment to assess the group. Watching

from behind him, I could see that only Hank and Clive looked a little nervous. Everyone else met Dad's eyes head-on with sad but determined expressions.

"My son is going to be heading up the investigation, which means that I'll be kept informed throughout. Deputy Marks will be assisting him. But if any of you have concerns or questions, feel free to contact me directly," Dad told them. Normally, he would never have suggested that someone go around one of his investigators and talk to him directly, but this was an election year and he couldn't afford to ignore the politics where a family as prominent as the Parrishes was involved. "I'm going to leave the questioning to them right now. Please answer as completely as you can," he told them all.

"When will they release our father's body?" Joe asked.

"As soon as the coroner is satisfied that he's gotten all the answers he can. My guess would be in two to four days," Dad told him and Joe nodded thoughtfully.

"What… happened to him?" Marge asked. They clearly wanted answers from the top.

"All I can tell you right now is that it appears to be a deliberate act by an unknown person."

Everyone looked surprised, though they had to have already known from the way we were acting that this wasn't an accident.

"Murder," Jane said like a character in a movie.

"We'll know more in a couple of days, but we have to proceed with that assumption." A crisis brought out Dad's best media-speak.

Everyone seemed mollified for the moment. Dad said his goodbyes, then pulled me out into the hallway and whispered, "Got a call from Jamie on my way over here." Jamie was the frequent babysitter for Dad's spoiled, one-hundred-and-ninety-pound, black-and-white Great Dane. "Mauser doesn't seem to be feeling very well, so I've got to run him over to the vet. But call me if you need anything."

Back in the living room I took Darlene aside. "For this

first interview, let's split up."

She seemed to consider this for a minute, then said, "I'll take Clive, Hank Junior and Andrew."

I squinted at her. I realized she'd seen the same things I had in Junior and Clive, but there was no way I was letting her question the two most interesting members of the family.

"I'll take Hank, Joe and Marge," I countered. I glanced over at the group, but they were busy talking amongst themselves and didn't seem to notice us negotiating over the interviews.

"Leaving me with Clive, Andrew and Jane?" She thought for a moment. "Deal."

I shook my head, wondering how I'd gotten myself into the position of bargaining with someone who'd joined our department less than two weeks earlier.

Joe offered to let us use the dining room and office for the interviews. I took the dining room. I decided to let Hank Junior stew a little bit and started with the oldest brother.

Joe said that he'd been with different employees all morning. I wrote down all the names, planning to check his alibi carefully as he seemed to be the one most likely to benefit from his father's death.

He wasted a few minutes trying to get information out of me about what had actually happened to Hank Senior. I fended him off and asked, "Can you think of anyone that would have wanted to hurt your father?"

He sat back and appeared to think about it. "Not really."

"You all do a lot of business in the county. Were there ever any financial disputes that got hot?"

"Dad didn't make enemies. Now my grandfather was a different story. Grandpa would fight anyone over a penny. In fact, Dad said it was because of Grandpa that he didn't have to be meaner with folks. Grandpa had scared everyone so bad that no one dared try to cheat us. Of course, there were people that Dad didn't like and that he wouldn't do business with. He was a good judge of folks, and there were people he didn't want around the farm or the family."

Joe stopped talking, but I could tell that he was thinking about something. I let the silence grow until he decided to fill me in.

"Now this was a long time ago, but the closest thing to a real enemy he ever made was a kid by the name of Joel something… Joel Patrick. I think he was from Panama City or somewhere down on the Gulf."

"What'd your dad have against him? When was this?"

"Almost twenty years ago, maybe? This kid started hanging around Jane. It was her fault as much as his, probably. She… Anyway, she'd met him on a spring break trip to Panama City and he just followed her back up here."

"Your dad didn't like him hanging around Jane? Why?" Most fathers automatically don't like guys tagging after their daughters, but I got the feeling there was more to this story.

"Dad was pretty protective of both my sisters. More so of Jane because she needed more protecting. But this kid was weird. We were already cutting hay that year and Dad thought that he could scare Joel away by giving him a job with me in the fields. Dad told me to work him till he dropped. But the guy was tough. Joel was thin, didn't look like he'd have any strength, but it turned out he'd spent most his time on the water sailing and boarding and stuff, so the sun and hard work didn't bother him."

"So what was wrong with him?"

"He wasn't very dependable. Showed up late half the time, and the other half of the time he'd get there before me and be trying to do something he couldn't. But what was really odd was what he talked about. All kinds of strange stuff about philosophers and crap. I went to college, graduated with an MBA, I can talk about Nietzsche or Freud. But he would mix it all up, kind of come up with his own theories. Most of them could be summed up as 'Joel is better than anyone else.'"

"But the work didn't scare him off?"

"No, but Dad's plan still had the desired effect. With Joel

working on the farm, Jane got bored with him. In two weeks she'd told him to move on."

"How'd he take that?"

"Like any guy ever. Kicked stuff, cussed a little and lurked around for a couple of days until Dad went out and gave him a talking-to. That's when things got a little rough. The kid hit Dad. I wasn't there, so I can't say how provoked Joel was, but at some point he slugged Dad in the face. Jane saw the fight. According to her, it was over four seconds after that punch landed."

"He knocked your dad out?"

Joe almost smiled and shook his head. "Not a chance. Dad spent a couple tours in Vietnam. Before Joel could react, Dad had him face down on the ground and was on his back, holding his head up. Jane told me that Dad had already pulled his pocketknife out and was opening it with his teeth when she got to him and started tugging on his arm. She was sure Dad was having some sort of flashback and was going to slit Joel's throat. But he came to his senses and let the boy up. Jane said Joel ran about twenty feet away and cussed Dad out, threatening him. But none of us ever saw him again."

"How'd Jane feel about all that?"

"Actually, she seemed to calm down a little. Had a little more respect for Dad after that." Joe shrugged.

I questioned him about their employees, but he said there hadn't been any recent turnover and no one had been fired in years.

"Can you and Hank drive a tractor?" I asked.

He looked at me with a crooked smile. "Ha! Are you kidding? All four of us kids learned to drive a small tractor with a bush hog by the time we were twelve. Once we were in high school we were allowed to run the big one with a bailer. Not just me and Hank, but the girls too. Dad thought everyone should be able to work a field. Why?"

I debated whether I should mention the stolen equipment, but decided the potential benefits of bringing it up outweighed the risks. "We found a backhoe in the woods near where your father's body was discovered. Would any of your people have a reason to be digging back there?" I asked.

"One of our backhoes?" Joe seemed genuinely puzzled.

"We don't think so. Can you think of any reason why anyone would be digging in those woods?" I asked again.

For just the briefest of moments I saw something in his expression, but it faded quickly. "No. No idea," he said and looked away.

"We'll need to account for everyone's movements this morning. Don't give your staff a heads-up. Let us talk to them," I said. "Oh, one more thing. Who inherits?"

Joe seemed momentarily taken aback, but quickly regained his composure. "I inherit the farm and the business capital. Marge, Jane and Hank will receive sizable amounts that have already been set aside," he told me.

I asked him to send Marge in next. Her eyes were red from crying, and she continually reached up to touch the small silver crucifix she wore around her neck. Like her father, nothing about her suggested that she came from a wealthy family. She sat down across from me and looked at me through eyes that seemed lost.

"Why? Why would anyone hurt Daddy?" she asked me.

"That's what I want to find out. I'm hoping that your family can help us."

"No one disliked him. You and your dad know that. He was a good man. Ask anyone." Her voice was begging me for answers. Unlike her brother Joe, who seemed able to compartmentalize his grief, Marge was reeling from the blow.

"I know. I liked and respected your father. And I really appreciated all the support he gave Dad when we lost my mother. We'll find the person who did this. But you're going to have to help me," I said, trying to get her to focus. "Please try and think. Is there anyone, even if it was from years ago, that might have wanted to hurt your dad?"

She squeezed her eyes shut and her brow furrowed for a few minutes as she considered the question.

"No, I just can't. He fired a few people over the years, and sometimes we had some vandalism, but no, I really can't think of anyone that would be mad enough at him to hurt him." Marge was the very definition of sincere.

"What about a guy named Joel?" I asked.

"Joel?" Her voice was puzzled.

"An old boyfriend of Jane's," I prodded.

"Maybe. Years ago. Jane has always had more boyfriends than you could shake a stick at. I used to be jealous of her when I was younger, but now I can see that those looks are a curse, not a blessing."

"So you don't remember a Joel? It would have been when your sister was about eighteen."

"Oh, I was in Gainesville then. University of Florida, getting my teaching degree. Secondary science," she said, reminding me that she was a teacher at Adams County High School.

"Were you at school this morning?"

"Yes, by seven every school morning. I like to have time to get my lessons ready," Marge stated.

I didn't press her on it. Assuming that someone couldn't be the murderer is almost always a mistake, but you can't give everyone equal weight as a suspect in a case like this where you're having to cast a wide net. I'd check up on the alibi at some point, just to be sure, but that could be reserved for downtime.

"Daddy always carried too much cash on him," Marge mentioned suddenly. "Maybe someone robbed him." I didn't tell her that his wallet was still in his back pocket with five hundred and twenty dollars in it.

"We're going to look into every possibility," I said, thanking her and asking her to send in Hank Junior.

He walked into the room and looked around like he expected to be jumped by invisible assailants. His eyes darted back and forth, and his hands never stopped moving. When he sat down, he just perched on the edge of the chair. I was still amazed at how much he looked like his father, though a much harder version. During my more than two years on patrol I got to where I could spot an addict, and Hank certainly had that lean and hungry look.

"You're nervous," I stated, trying to sound more sympathetic than adversarial.

"Let's cut the BS. You know that I've been in trouble for drinking and fighting." He paused, finding the next hard to admit. "And for possession." I could have added check and prescription fraud.

"Yes, and you can give me a little credit for knowing that a man who has gotten into trouble for being an addict and a dumbass isn't necessarily a killer, especially one that would kill his own father. As far as I'm concerned, you are no more a suspect than your brother or your sisters." The last was a bit of a white lie.

He looked down at his hands. "What you don't know is that I've been sober for fifty-three days. Not much, I know. But I was sober for four months before that. I've been trying. Dad and I were getting along better than we have in… hell, decades."

"Good for you," I said and meant it. "But you understand that I still have to ask you some questions."

He nodded, still looking down at his hands. "I want you to punish the man that killed him. I really do. And to answer your first question, I was in the garage—well, my room above the garage—asleep this morning until about nine o'clock. Dad didn't really understand, but my sponsor told me that if I could sleep, really sleep, it was a good sign and I should embrace it. Being able to sleep means I'm learning to live with who I was and what I've done in the past."

"Can anyone vouch for you?"

Hank sighed. "Maybe Dad's housekeeper. Maria something… her last name is unpronounceable. But the kitchen and laundry room are in the back, and she spends most of her time there before ten in the morning. Usually when I come down she shouts good morning to me."

"Did Maria see you come down this morning?"

"Maybe… I think so…"

I made a note to ask her about it when we questioned the employees, but he was right; if she wasn't sitting there all morning staring at the garage he could have left and come back without her seeing him. Hank seemed like he was being honest, but addicts are great liars. Most of them start practicing as soon as they start drinking or taking drugs.

"Who inherits your father's property?" I asked. I believed Joe, but I was curious what Hank would say.

"Joe gets the majority—the farm and the main house—and then Marge and Jane get a share. Dad also put money in a trust for me. Marge is in charge of that," Hank said sheepishly. "You can ask all of them. Dad and I talked about it, and we both agreed that I shouldn't have direct control of the money. Ten years ago, I would have been royally pissed about that. Sober, I have enough sense to know that my dark side can't be trusted. I'm better off if temptation is kept at arm's length."

We finished up and, after making a few notes, I followed him out into the hall. I got started on the employees while Darlene finished up with Jane. Almost all of the employees could provide alibis for the others. The few that had only partial alibis seemed very unlikely suspects.

Darlene helped with the last of the employees, then we took a short break to compare notes on the family before we headed back to the crime scene. I filled her in on Hank's problems, the inheritance and the fact that all of the family reportedly could drive a backhoe.

"What'd you come up with?" I asked her.

"Clive's a nice guy, Andrew's a jerk and Jane's a piece of work," Darlene said succinctly. "And they all agreed that no one in the world could have wanted to kill Mr. Hank Parrish Senior. Interestingly, Jane didn't mention a rogue boyfriend."

"The incident happened a long time ago and maybe she didn't think her boyfriend was serious. She would have known the guy better than any of the others."

"Maybe," Darlene said. "Jane and Clive gave me the same

information you got about the inheritance, while Andrew claimed to know nothing about it. And they all had alibis that will need to be checked. No smoking guns here."

"I'm not surprised. That backhoe is the fly in the ointment," I said as we got in the car. "If the murder was premeditated, that would explain the backhoe."

"But that's pretty lame. Everyone knew where Hank Senior was going to be working this morning. If he'd disappeared, there would have been a massive search and the freshly turned earth would have been discovered. We'd have brought in search dogs too, and they wouldn't have been fooled by a few feet of dirt, or even ten feet of dirt."

"On the bright side, the backhoe gives us a whole bunch of opportunities to recover trace evidence," I said. "And an alternative line of inquiry."

When we got back to the scene, there were only half a dozen tired-looking deputies still there, along with Marcus and Shantel.

"You two follow me," Shantel said without preamble. The sun was getting low in the sky. I looked at my watch to see that it was already six o'clock.

Shantel led us to a spot about ten feet inside the tree line. I could look through the trees and see where the holes had been dug and, when I turned around, I could see the spot twenty yards away where Parrish's body had been found in the field.

Shantel pulled out her phone and showed us a picture of a small feather lying in the dirt. "Don't worry, we took better pictures with the big camera. We found this right here." She pointed to a small yellow flag stuck in the ground.

"Part of the fletching from the bolt that killed Parrish?" I asked. I'd been fascinated with crossbows in high school.

"You got it on the first guess," Shantel said.

"So this is where our killer took his shot," Darlene said, looking around at the ground and bushes.

"We've picked this place apart for possible trace evidence. We won't know if we got anything for a while. We weren't lucky enough to find a branch with blood on it or anything that obvious."

"These days, even bad guys are smart enough not to toss around cigarette butts," I bemoaned.

A tow truck arrived to take the trailer and backhoe to our impound lot, where Shantel and Marcus could take a more in-depth look at it. Darlene and I helped wrap things up at the scene, then headed back to the office. We came up with a schedule for the next day that involved running down alibis and digging into the backgrounds of the family and employees, as well as talking to other people around the county about Parrish and any possible enemies he may have had.

I texted my girlfriend, Cara Laursen, before I left the station and told her I'd be over in about an hour. I wanted to talk with her as soon as possible about Marcy. I'd hoped my ex would leave town, or at least stay away from me, so I could avoid explaining all the messy details of my past to Cara, but apparently I wasn't going to be that lucky.

CHAPTER FOUR

My gate was open when I pulled into my driveway, which wasn't right. I tried to think back to that morning. Had I closed and locked it as I usually did? Probably. Maybe. Nothing is harder than trying to remember whether you did something that you always do. Routines are routines so you don't have to think about what you're doing.

I lived in an older doublewide on twenty acres about five miles outside of town. My house sat close to the center of the mostly wooded property, in a clearing that boasted half a dozen enormous old live oak trees. I parked in my usual spot and sat in the car for ten minutes while my eyes adjusted to the dark. Nothing moved or looked out of the ordinary. I pulled out my flashlight, but didn't turn it on. Reaching up, I clicked off the dome light so I wouldn't lose my night vision or illuminate myself as I stepped out of my car. Once outside, I took my Glock from its holster and began to approach the house with the flashlight still off. The sky was clear and the half moon provided a fair bit of light.

Everything appeared normal. I moved around the side of the house, only occasionally tripping over deadfall. When I got to the back of the house I saw a broken window in my office. Sighing, I headed for the back door. I pressed my ear to the door and waited. Next, I tapped on the door and listened again. *Enough of this*, I thought and opened the door, gun at the ready across the wrist of my left hand that held the flashlight. I thumbed a light switch and peered through the doorway, checking both sides of the doorjamb. Nothing.

I entered the house and went room to room, concentrating on clearing it before I worried about what might have been stolen. Once I was sure no one was hiding, I turned on all the lights, closed the back door and looked for Ivy, the tabby cat I'd rescued from the streets last year. I found her curled up on top of the refrigerator. She looked down at me accusingly, as though I'd failed in my mission to provide her with a safe and secure home.

"This wouldn't have happened if you could bark," I told her.

I noticed a half-empty beer bottle sitting on the kitchen counter. *Okay, we probably have some DNA evidence. That's good,* I thought.

I went back through all the rooms again. The house had been thoroughly searched, but nothing much seemed to have been taken. The only thing missing was about a hundred dollars I kept in my nightstand.

A prickly feeling ran across my skin. *Marcy.* I went back into the kitchen and looked more closely at the beer bottle. Red lipstick covered the top. I sniffed the bottle. It even smelled like her.

I could feel the blood pound in my temples. Of all the luck. Why did she have to come back to town now? And why was she picking on me? The answer was easy. She loved to get under my skin. The real question was: what was I going to do about it?

I needed to tell Cara. After feeding Ivy and reassuring her that I'd do a better job in the future, I boarded up the office window as best I could and locked up the house. Next I went to the small shed where I kept my lawn and power tools and found a heavier chain and a hardcore padlock for the front gate. The horse might be gone, but I was going to make sure the barn door was well secured.

As I drove, I thought about calling Cara to warn her about Marcy, but I didn't want to get into a big discussion about it over the phone. Did Marcy even know about Cara? How crazy *was* she these days? Obviously crazy enough to break into my house.

When I pulled into Cara's driveway, everything seemed normal. She lived in the east half of a duplex that she rented from a nice older couple. But as I got out of the car, I noticed that it was very quiet. *It's just your overactive imagination*, I told my inner voice. *You just got burgled, dumbass*, the inner voice reminded me.

When I got to the door, I didn't hear a TV, but Cara usually preferred to read after work. I raised my hand to knock, but then I heard something loud thump against the inside of the door. I froze. Was someone lurking on the other side? Was Marcy already spreading her chaos to Cara's doorstep?

I leaned in and put my ear to the door. The house had a typical modern construction and, while the door was made of steel, it was hollow so sounds were easily transferred from inside. Sure enough, I could hear movement and breathing. Deep, heavy breathing. Certainly not Cara's.

I couldn't think of any reason why Cara would be leaning against the inside of the door. If she used the peephole, she'd have seen it was me. Maybe she was playing some practical joke on me? *Not really her style*, I thought.

I considered my options. I had a key, so even if the door was locked I could still get in through the front door. But if someone was just inside the door, I could have been walking into a fight where I didn't have all the facts. Important facts, like where Cara was, how many people were inside and how well armed they were. I rejected going in the front door.

I could call her. That wasn't a bad option. I snuck away from the front door and pulled out my phone, but there was no answer. I moved up next to the door and called again. I couldn't hear the phone ringing, but again I heard movement inside. I could almost sense a person leaning against the inside of the door.

I was starting to feel frustrated and anxious. Checking all the doors and windows was my next choice. I started around Cara's side of the building, but unfortunately she had most of her blinds down. This was also normal, but not helpful. I crept up to the back door that opened out onto a small patio with a utility closet. I knew the door led into her kitchen. It was a cottage door, with the top half made up of a series of small windows. From a security standpoint, this was awful, but at least the deadbolt required a key on both sides so someone couldn't break a single small pane and reach in and unlock the door.

I slipped my key into the lock and slowly turned it. I knew I was going to make some noise, but you'd have to have a really good set of ears to hear it. Once the door was unlocked, I turned the knob slowly and pushed gently until the door was slightly ajar.

I stopped and took a deep breath. Was I overreacting? Probably, but with anything that might involve Marcy, I'd rather err on the side of caution. I pulled my gun out and reminded myself to keep my finger well clear of the trigger guard. I didn't want to make any mistakes that I'd regret later. Set, I pushed the door open and entered the kitchen.

I hadn't gone two feet from the door when a large black figure raced into the kitchen straight at me. I started to raise my gun, but time had run out. I was thrown hard against the cabinets and went sprawling on the floor. I heard a shout from the other room.

I still had my gun in my hand, but I was pinned to the floor. Only then did I realize that the hot breath of my attacker smelled oddly of Pepto-Bismol. The lights came on, exposing the identity of my assailant. It was Mauser, my father's overgrown, two-year-old monster of a Great Dane.

"What are you doing?!" yelled Cara.

Mauser and I both looked at her.

"I'm trying to keep him from getting worked up," she

said, sounding a bit peeved as I managed to re-holster my gun. Meanwhile, Mauser danced up and down on top of me and, looking straight into my face, gave me one of his signature seismic barks.

"Now you bark. If you'd done that fifteen minutes ago all of this could have been avoided," I explained to Mauser.

"Why the hell were you sneaking in the back door with your gun out?" Cara asked.

"I… came over to… It's complicated." I looked at Mauser as he tried to lick my face. "What are *you* doing here?" I asked him. "Move, get off," I told him as I got up off the floor. I could see Alvin, Cara's Pug, peering in from the living room at the circus. I closed the outer door and tried to regain some of my dignity.

We went into the living room with Mauser prancing beside me, my arm held gently in his mouth as though I was his trophy burglar. We settled on the couch and managed to convince Mauser to lay on the floor with Alvin, who was still looking very puzzled by all of the commotion.

"Okay, you first, why is Mauser here?" I asked quickly.

"That's pretty simple. Your dad brought Mauser into the vet with an upset tummy and was wondering what he was going to do with him tonight while he went to some campaign event. Apparently his regular sitter had class, so I offered to keep him here for the night. Your turn. What was with all the sneaking around?"

"Okay, long story. First, I have to tell you something I've been avoiding." I took a deep breath. "I have a slightly demented ex. She lives down in south Florida now, but her dad's been sick. Actually, he's in hospice care, so she's here visiting."

"I figured you had ex-girlfriends." She squinted. "How crazy?"

"That's why I was sneaking in your back door. She broke into my house this afternoon. I heard old big-hooves here," I indicated the sacked-out Great Dane at our feet, "and thought someone was in your house."

"That sounds like a stretch."

"Okay, I admit it, some of her crazy tends to rub off on me. She… Her name is Marcy. She came by the Donut Hole today while Darlene and I were having lunch. Marcy wanted some stuff she thought she'd left with me when she moved out." Right after I said those words the atmosphere felt awkward. Cara and I had gotten to the point where we'd exchanged keys and had frequent sleepovers, but we hadn't yet seriously discussed moving in with each other.

"And you really thought she might have broken in here?" Cara sounded genuinely surprised by the idea.

"Did I mention she could be a little… extreme?"

"How long ago did you all break up?"

"Long before I went to the law enforcement academy. About nine years ago." We were on to the *what-did-you-do-with-her-and-how-long-did-you-do-it?* stage of the conversation, exactly what I'd hoped to avoid since I'd found out Marcy was in town.

"How long were you…?" Cara caught herself. "I guess that isn't really any of my business," she said, but everything in her tone suggested that she desperately wanted to know.

"I don't mind talking about my ups and many downs with Marcy. I had a crush on her during high school, but I wasn't cool enough for her so nothing happened until later. I told you how I left college in Georgia to be with Dad after Mom died and I never went back. But when Dad decided to run for sheriff, I figured it wouldn't hurt to at least finish up my AA, so I enrolled at Tallahassee Community College. I ran into Marcy there… Actually, I think she purposely ran into me. I think she needed a regular ride to school, since both of us were still living over here.

"Naively, I was all excited about the chance to spend time with my old crush. To be fair, she'd had a couple of hard bumps in her life at that point. She'd gone from being the hot fish in the small pond to being one of the many fish swimming around in the real world. Also, her life at home wasn't going so great. Her mom and dad had issues. Long and short of it, we ended up living together for two good months and nine progressively worse ones."

"And now she came back and broke into your house?" Cara asked, sounding understandably skeptical.

"Crazy is as crazy does," I threw out, then realized I was being too flippant. "Honestly, I don't know what she wants. I told her I didn't have anything of hers. I moved out of the apartment shortly after she did, plus another time or two since then."

"You're sure that it was Marcy that broke into your house?" Cara asked.

"Positive. One of her habits that bugged me the most was leaving glasses and bottles all over the place. She left a beer bottle on the counter, and there was lipstick on it. Besides, nothing was taken except some cash."

"Are you going to talk to her?"

That was a loaded question, but I was determined to be honest with Cara now that it was out in the open. Of course I didn't want to talk with Marcy again, but she wasn't one to stop digging once she got something into her head. "I need to. Though I don't know how I'm going to prove a negative."

"Is there any chance that you *do* have something of hers?" Cara asked reasonably.

"I appreciate you taking this so… unemotionally," I said.

"We haven't gotten to the emotional part yet," she said in a tone that let me know that somewhere along the way I'd stepped in it. Then she enlightened me. "I'm a bit ticked off that you waited this long to tell me that your rogue ex-girlfriend was roaming the countryside." There was a slight edge to her voice.

"I'm sorry. My relationship with her was so long ago I just figured she'd moved past it. She's here because her father is dying, so I didn't think there'd be any reason I'd have to talk to her. Trust me, I've been trying to avoid running into her for weeks."

Cara punched me on the shoulder. "Talk to me, and I'll

try not to overreact." She hesitated and then added, with a smile in her voice, "I did say 'try', so no guarantees."

"To answer your earlier question, I'm pretty sure that I don't have any of her stuff. Though I do remember leaving a few boxes over at Dad's house. I might go check them out. I put them there when I moved out of the apartment I shared with Marcy, and I haven't looked at them since."

"Are you going to confront Marcy?"

"Not right away," I said, which seemed to satisfy Cara and end the awkward former girlfriend conversation.

We settled down on the couch with Alvin, which led to a jealous Mauser trying to edge his big butt up on the furniture as well. Cara asked about the rest of my day and I gave her the broad outlines of the Parrish murder without any details that wouldn't be in the papers tomorrow. I also took a few minutes to whine about Darlene.

Before I eventually said goodbye, we spent the better part of an hour watching Tyrannosaurus Dog try to cope with the more playful Pug. When Mauser was particularly annoyed, he'd take one of his enormous paws and pin the small dog to the ground until Alvin managed to squirm out from underneath and come charging back to lick Mauser's face some more. You had to admire the little guy's guts.

CHAPTER FIVE

Even though I got to the office half an hour early, Darlene was already at her desk when I came in. "Good morning, sunshine. I'm making a list of the people we need to interview," she told me without looking up.

I ignored her and texted Pete, catching him before he left his house. We agreed to meet for lunch. I planned on ditching Darlene sometime before that.

"I'm going out to collect surveillance footage from the route that our backhoe thief would have taken," I told her.

"There are only five cameras that had a chance of catching his car on the road and I picked up the footage from them last night," she said, still working on her list.

My first plan ruined, I asked, "So who's on your list?" My new plan was to suggest that we split up the interviews.

"I've got about a dozen people who knew Parrish. Those will probably be quick ones. Ask them if he had any enemies, had he been acting differently, what about his family. The hope is that we can get a line on someone with a motive."

She told me this as if I didn't know what kind of questions we needed to ask. *Don't let her get under your skin*, I told myself as I let her do just that.

"The murder could have been random," I said, then

threw in, "Not driven by a motive," trying to imply that she didn't know what a random murder meant. But she never seemed to notice when I was trying to annoy her.

"You're forgetting the holes. Someone probably took that backhoe out there to dig a grave."

I hadn't forgotten the holes. "The holes mean something, but we don't know what," I said, even though I thought there was a good possibility that Darlene was right. Why else would the killer steal the machine and go dig holes in the woods?

"If not graves, what? Did he steal it and plan on meeting a buyer out there? Maybe the holes were to demonstrate what the backhoe was capable of? But that doesn't make sense. Anyone who wanted to buy it would know what it could do. If it was a used one, you might need to show someone that it worked. But that was a brand new machine," Darlene said thoughtfully.

"What if Parrish was going to buy it and the deal went bad?" I was just throwing ideas around, but this one had some merit. Except that I couldn't imagine Mr. Parrish buying stolen goods.

Mercifully, Darlene agreed to split up the morning's interviews with the folks that had known Parrish. But the interviews yielded absolutely zero new information. Everyone we talked to, including his minister, his doctor and lifelong friends said some version of the same thing: "He was the best guy in the world. I just can't believe someone would kill him." I'd never had a victim be referred to with that much universal love. Parrish seemed to be the lovechild of Jimmy Carter and Mother Teresa.

After my last interview, I called Dr. Darzi in Tallahassee. He hadn't conducted the autopsy yet, but a preliminary examination confirmed the obvious: the victim had died from a crossbow bolt that pierced his eye and went through his brain.

"I doubt that the autopsy is going to tell us much more," Darzi said. "Toxicology, maybe. We'll see. I can tell you that the bolt's trajectory looks flat, so it was not a long shot. I'll have to look at data to give you a range. I don't see any signs that the killer came in contact with the victim, but we'll be thorough as always. If there are any prints or other trace evidence, we'll let you know."

I called Darlene and shared Darzi's comments with her. She said she had a lunch appointment in Tallahassee, so I suggested that she check in with Darzi that afternoon if she wanted.

Pete was sitting at one of the outdoor tables when I pulled up at Deep Pit Bar-b-que. The weather was nice with clear blue skies and a cool breeze.

I joined him after getting my lunch. "How are the girls?" I asked as he finished sending a text on his phone. Parenting in the twenty-first century.

"Jenny's driving and Kim wants to be a cop like her old man." He shrugged. "Jenny is the one I worry about. I told her no phones on in the car, period. I want her phone off and in the back seat. I've seen enough accidents caused by texting." He shuddered, like a bear shaking off a particularly bad nightmare. I resisted any comments about pots and kettles, knowing how concerned he was about his daughter.

He took a bite of his sandwich and asked, "How are you and Darl getting along?"

I groaned. "Honestly, she's a good investigator. It's all those little personal quirks that drive me crazy. Not that you didn't piss me off with your incessant texting," I joked.

"Screw you too," he said with a laugh. "Personally, I'm glad I'm not on the Parrish case with you. There's going to be some serious pressure if you don't have a suspect soon."

"Tell me something I don't already know." I gave him a quick overview of the case, then finished with, "Why would someone dig holes in *those* woods?" I added the emphasis because I didn't think that it was a random choice.

Pete ate the last bite of his sandwich, then leaned back on

the bench. "To bury the body," he said.

"We've been up and down that road," I sighed. "It's possible, but the more I look at the case, the less I like that answer. But I do think that the backhoe is the key. Why was it there?"

"You dig holes either to bury something or to dig something up," Pete said simply.

"Dig something up. Maybe."

"Have you found a motive?"

"For someone to kill the Adams County equivalent of Mr. Rogers? No. That's why I'm focusing on the backhoe."

"Guess he wasn't having an affair." Pete smiled.

"No. Nor was he stealing, dealing drugs or growing drugs."

"Something in his past?"

"Maybe. But if you hate someone enough to come back years later to kill him, you'd think you'd do it in a way that's more personal than a crossbow from twenty yards away."

"Good point," Pete allowed. "Mistaken identity?"

"I think the shot was too close for that, but Hank Senior and Hank Junior *do* look a bit alike. And Hank Junior has been on the buying end of a fair share of drugs. But if someone wanted to kill Junior, they'd probably know him well enough to realize he's not going to be working a hay field at that time of the morning."

After a while I told Pete about Marcy breaking into my place.

"I'm glad that I was chubby and unattractive growing up. Saves me from being haunted by ex-girlfriends." Pete chuckled.

"I didn't have that many. Unfortunately, I got tangled up with the thirty-two-pounder of loose cannons."

"Where Mr. Parrish's body was found… Was it close to the railroad tracks?" Pete shifted back to the murder.

"Not too far. A couple trains went by while we were there. Good point. I'll see if I can find out what trains went by before, and possibly during, the murder."

"Good luck. I had a dead body near the tracks in town a couple of years ago and contacting the right guy at the right office at the right company took a week. I should be able to give you the contact numbers I got back then, though the chances they'll work now are iffy at best. Besides, they only have one or two guys on those freight trains."

We talked about his cases—a drug deal gone bad that had left an innocent bystander dead and a serial carjacker. "It's just a matter of time before he jacks the wrong car and somebody ends up shot," Pete grumbled as he stood up and headed for his car.

I waved as he left, then called Joe Parrish and asked if he'd mind talking with me again.

I met Joe Parrish down at the dirt drive that led to the clearing where we found the backhoe.

"Thanks for meeting me," I said, shaking his hand. I always appreciated people who didn't clam up or lawyer up when they found themselves in the middle of an investigation though, sadly, that's exactly the advice I would have given to anyone who found themselves in such a situation. Too many state attorneys and investigators focus on the information they have and the people they have access to rather than going out and fighting for the information they really need. Arresting someone is not always the same as solving a case.

"Anything I can do to get the man who murdered Dad." His voice was quiet and cold.

"I want to show you something." I had a hunch that Joe knew something he wasn't telling me yesterday when we were talking about these woods. I'd looked on the property appraiser's website and was able to determine that the area between the train tracks, the field and the road was about twenty acres.

I started walking toward the spot where we found the backhoe. "Do you ever use this land for anything?" I asked as we walked.

"Not really. It's low and pretty swampy. Mostly it's wildlife habitat. We've got a tree stand near the tracks. Winter mornings, deer will come out of the woods where they've been bedded down, looking for forage. I took my first deer from that stand when I was twelve. A six-point."

We came to the spot where the backhoe and trailer had been found. They were gone now, but the ground was all chewed up and muddy.

"This is where we found the backhoe. Can you think of any reason why someone would have brought it down here?" I asked him again, watching his face. His brows furrowed in confusion.

"No. It was just sitting on the trailer?"

"More or less." I didn't want to give away too many details. I started walking again, following the trail left by the backhoe.

When we came to the area where the machine had dug the holes, Joe Parrish stopped and stared. His face had an odd look. I couldn't discern the mix of emotions.

"Do you know why someone would come out here and dig holes?" I asked, feeling like a broken record.

Joe didn't answer. He was staring out beyond the woods now, toward the spot where his father had died. He walked over to the edge of the woods until he was standing close to the spot where we had found the feather. He looked out at the tractor, still parked in the field, and at a spot nearby where the grass was discolored.

"Is that where it happened?"

"Yes."

"I'm glad he didn't suffer," Joe said in a flat tone.

"If you know something about these woods, your father or the murder, now would be the time to tell me," I encouraged him. *Should I take the gloves off? Put some pressure on him?* I wondered.

He still didn't say anything. He just kept staring at the spot where his father had been struck down.

"There is no one else here. Anything you tell me would be your word against mine. If you know something, give me some indication of which way to look," I prodded.

Joe turned abruptly. "I'll get someone to come down in the morning and finish cutting the field," he said, more to himself than to me, then started walking back toward our cars.

Standing by his truck, he turned and looked me straight in the eyes. "Dad trusted your father. I know you're going to do your best to solve this… atrocity. No one wants that more than me. If I have information that will help you, I'll tell you."

He started to get in the truck, but I put my hand on the door and stopped him. "Talk to me. Let me be the judge."

"Dad always said there was only one judge, and justice couldn't be delivered in this world. I guess we'll find out," he said, staring over my shoulder.

What the hell do you say to that? I thought. All I could do was take my hand off of the door and let him get in the truck and drive away.

CHAPTER SIX

I was passing the Fast Mart on Jefferson when I saw Marcy's car. I quickly went over the pros and cons of confronting her about the break-in and decided that the best thing to do would be to let it go. So, of course, I turned around and pulled into the parking lot.

I could see her through the store window, standing at the counter buying something. But my attention was distracted when I noticed there was someone slumped down in the passenger seat of her car. I pulled in alongside it and got out.

I tapped on the window. The figure crouched down lower in the seat, as if he was trying to ooze out through the floor of the car. I knocked harder. Finally he looked up and I motioned for him to lower the window.

"Hi," he mumbled after lowering the glass.

"You didn't bother to let me know you were back in town, and now I find you in Marcy's car?" I scolded him.

"I met her down in Miami, that's all." Eddie Thompson, my cross-dressing confidential informant, stared down at his lap, looking as guilty as a puppy caught chewing on a slipper.

I looked back at the store and could see Marcy arguing with the cashier. I could have told the poor man that he'd lose. I turned back to Eddie.

"You're my CI. You need to let me know when you come and go."

"Marcy told me who your new partner is. I don't want to work for you anymore."

"I don't know what you have against Deputy Marks—"

His head jerked up and he interrupted me. "She's a catty bitch. She arrested me once for drugs. When she found out I was wearing a bra, she started laughing. She even started making jokes about it with another officer with me standing right there. I quit." He slumped back down in the seat, arms crossed.

I glanced at the store to make sure Marcy was still inside. She and the cashier were both swinging their arms around and arguing.

"You can't quit, and what's more, you're going to keep an eye on Marcy for me. I want a report later today on what's she's doing, and I want regular follow-ups. This is non-optional."

"But she's a friend," he whined.

"You've never hesitated to inform on friends and family before. A fact that I would guess you'd still want kept a secret."

Pouting, he grumbled, "I could use some money."

I took out a twenty and dropped it in his lap. "Report on Marcy tonight," I told him and got in my car, leaving before Marcy finished her verbal brawl with the poor clerk.

Before I was a mile down the road I heard dispatch send a deputy to help the Fast Mart clerk remove an unruly female customer from the store.

Back at the office I wrote up reports from my notes until Darlene came in around three o'clock. She had gone by the morgue and talked to Dr. Darzi after the autopsy. The only new information he'd come up with was a time of death based on Parrish's stomach contents, and all that did was confirm what we'd already concluded from the timeline provided by the family and employees.

I hesitated to tell her about my meeting with Joe, but I couldn't see the point in hiding it from her. I thought she might be irritated that I hadn't talked to her first, since he had to be considered a suspect. We knew he personally couldn't have murdered his father, but with an inheritance standing in the balance, it wasn't unheard of for someone to hire a hitman. But she took it in stride.

"Probably a good idea to try and get him aside and talk to him man-to-man out in the woods. He's definitely the Marlboro Man type."

I didn't tell her yet that he'd been acting strangely about those woods. I didn't have any concrete suspicions… just a gut feeling that Joe knew *something*.

I mentioned that I'd spread the BOLO on the truck that was used to steal the backhoe out to two hundred miles and tagged it as wanted in a murder investigation.

Darlene smiled at me. "I went out to three hundred on it, and I double checked the VIN in the report and online."

I was annoyed, but had to admit to myself that it was a smart move. Many a vehicle had slipped through the system because of data that wasn't entered correctly.

We went down to the evidence room where Marcus and Shantel were boxing up materials from a year-old arson case to send to the prosecutor. When they were done, we all went over the evidence that had been collected at the Parrish murder site.

"With the railroad tracks close by, we got a lot of trash. People walk up those tracks and throw their junk everywhere," Shantel said, looking at a box full of old potato chip bags and plastic bottles. Then she held up an evidence bag with a smaller jewel bag inside. "We got a few of these too."

"I don't think this is drug related," I said.

"What about the backhoe?" Darlene asked.

"We got a whole bunch of fingerprints off it. And I'm sure we got DNA too. But that thing was behind Mill's for a couple of months. Lord knows how many people touched it," Shantel said. Marcus, the quiet one of the pair, nodded in agreement.

"So what we have is a ton of evidence, but nothing that will help us find the killer," I said.

"On the bright side, find the killer and some of this will probably help put him in jail," Shantel said, waving at the boxes of evidence. "That's not to say we won't run the prints and DNA and see if they match anyone in the National Crime Information Center, but that's going to take a while."

I nodded, knowing that collecting and scanning all of the evidence was a huge task. One of the problems with an outdoor crime scene was that you had to sort through all of the non-evidence to find anything relevant. With this collection of items including so much drug paraphernalia, even if we got a hit we couldn't be sure that the felon had anything to do with our case.

"We'd better get to work," Darlene said with more cheer than I thought was warranted, but she was right. We each took a box and sat down, carefully examining the items and their tags. The idea was to give Shantel and Marcus some items of particular interest to focus on.

"What have you got?" Darlene asked me as I shoved my last box away. In front of me were five bags. She was carrying six of her own.

"Two fairly fresh cigarette butts found within fifty feet of the backhoe, a Big Thirst cup from the Fast Mart that looks fairly new, a piece of cloth found near the trailer and, last but certainly the most disgusting, a used condom found hanging off a bush within ten feet of the trailer."

"I've got a crack pipe, a Coke bottle, a rag, two cigarillo butts and a candy wrapper. The first four items were found on the trail between the trailer and the clearing, while one of the butts and the wrapper were close to where the holes were dug."

We handed these over to Marcus since Shantel had been called out to collect evidence at an auto burglary.

The sun was low in the sky by the time I left the office. I touched base with Cara and made plans to see her the next day. Tonight I needed to stop by Dad's place.

A cold front was supposed to move through during the night and rain was already beginning to fall by the time I parked in front of the house. The light was on in the barn when I got out of the car, but it went out almost immediately and I could see Dad running through the rain toward the house. He seemed to move a little awkwardly. I met him on the porch.

"You okay?" I asked him.

"What?"

"You were running a little stiff."

"That's called arthritis. If you just came by to remind me I'm getting old, you can leave now." He said it with a laugh, but there was an edge to his voice.

"I didn't mean to—"

"If you're lucky, you'll get old too. Come on, let's get inside."

There was no Mauser to greet us at the door, but a gruff bark from the living room told me that he'd had his dinner and was off duty for the day.

"He feeling better?"

"Yes, thank God. When he has stomach issues…" Dad shook his head, trying to fend off that horrid memory and thankfully not going into details.

"I really just came over to look at some stuff in the garage," I told Dad. "I think there are still some boxes of mine out there."

"They're in the far back corner. I can open the garage door and you can back your car in. I'll help you load them up."

"That's okay, I just want to see what's in them," I said.

"The hell you say. I've been moving those boxes around for the better part of a decade. Go get your car," Dad said, no compromise in his tone.

With the car pulled into the garage as far as Dad's tools and assorted half-finished projects would allow, I found the five liquor boxes with my name scrawled across them in black ink.

"With all the other stuff you have in here, I wouldn't think that my boxes were that big of a problem," I kidded him.

"I should have made you take them when you moved into your trailer. Come on." He grabbed one of the boxes and took it to my trunk.

With the steady drizzle of rain and as dark as it was, I had to concentrate as I drove home. Pulling up to my gate, I saw that the chain and lock were still in place. There were a couple of other dirt driveways within a hundred feet of mine, but there weren't any streetlights so I left my headlights on as I got out to open the gate.

I had just bent over and was trying to get the right key inserted in the lock when I heard an odd sound behind me. I started to turn my head when a voice came from beyond the light cast by my headlights.

"Don't move. I have a gun pointed at you." The voice was low and deep, but I got the impression that whoever it was had to make an effort to sound dangerous.

"What do you want?" I asked. I was still half bent over with rain running into my eyes, but I held my hands steady where the gunman could see them.

"You know what I want," was the completely unhelpful answer.

"I'm going to straighten up." I did it slowly.

"Damn it! Don't move. I'm not kidding you, I'll shoot."

I had my hands up in the air now. My mind was calculating how fast I could draw my gun and fire at the vague shadow twenty feet away. The light from my own headlights was keeping me from getting a clear view of him.

On the range I could draw and fire an accurate shot at this distance in a second and a half, but with the rain and the blinding lights, there was no guarantee.

"I have no idea what you're talking about. Tell me what you want and maybe we can work something out," I told him, hoping to get some more information about what was going on and who I was dealing with.

"I can't believe you're playing games," he spat out.

I could hear the sound of a pickup truck coming down the main road toward us, its headlights already lighting up the road.

"I can't help you if you don't tell me what you want," I said, stalling to give the truck time to get closer.

"I swear I'll shoot you dead if you don't give me—"

The truck was twenty feet away and coming fast. Now was my chance. As the vehicle whooshed by, I fell to the wet ground and drew my gun. I hesitated a second to allow the truck to pass before I fired a shot, but the dark figure jerked the trigger on his own gun and I fired back. His shot went wild and I was pretty sure mine had too. By the time I got to my feet, he was gone in the rain and the darkness.

I looked up and down the road, trying to decide which way he'd run. The shooter had to have had a vehicle. He wouldn't have walked the five miles from town. I started running in the direction of the nearest driveway only to get there and hear the sound of a truck start up in the opposite direction. I turned back in time to see the red taillights of a white dually drive away. The tag lights were out, so I didn't have a chance to get the number.

Panting, I stood in the road as water dripped off my hair and into my eyes. I holstered my gun and went back to my car.

CHAPTER SEVEN

By the time I reached the house I'd decided not to call out the crime scene techs. In the rain, any evidence that was out there would be long gone. The bullet he'd fired went high and off into a field, never to be found. I would write up a report, just for the record, but even the shot I fired wouldn't cause me any problems. I was off duty, on my own property, and the gun was mine. We had the option of carrying our personal guns, and the Glock I used was my own that I'd customized by replacing the trigger and adding night sights.

I fed Ivy and told her that she was going to have to up her guard cat game, or we were going to have to get a dog. She gave me a cold, dark look that made me glad that she couldn't talk.

I called Pete and asked him to bring over a couple of game cameras. I had two that I placed out in the woods, just to see what types of animals wandered by. Sometimes I'd bait them with old apples and end up with dozens of pictures of foxes or raccoons carting off the fruit. I knew that Pete, while not a hunter, kept a few for the same purpose. His girls had enjoyed the footage from the "critter cams" when they were younger.

After using a flashlight to collect my cameras from the

woods, I put them up at two strategic spots in the driveway. I was waiting for Pete at the gate when he drove up.

"Can't you ever have an emergency during business hours?" he grumbled. The sky was still dripping and now a cold wind was blowing out of the north.

Pete perked up after I explained everything that had gone down at the gate. We managed to find the spent shell casing ejected from the ambusher's gun. Guns leave marks on the cases that can be matched back to them, assuming we ever found a suspect. This casing was from a nine millimeter weapon, which wasn't a surprise. I bagged it and let Pete take charge of it. Next we set up the two cameras he'd brought on either side of the gate. I figured this was all probably too little too late, but I was tired of having my property disturbed.

"Hopefully if they find one camera, they won't find all of them," I said.

"This one is old. It even makes a little noise when it goes off, so maybe they'll just find that one. Whoever it is, they have to know you're going to take some precautions. Are you sure that it wasn't Marcy?"

"I'm sure. I'm even pretty sure that she didn't have anything to do with it. She's crazy, but not insane. Nor particularly violent."

"What about the break-in? Could the guy tonight have been the one who broke into your house?" Pete asked.

"I thought about that, but the break-in fit Marcy's MO. Especially right after she'd asked me if I had anything of hers." As I said this, I remembered the boxes in my trunk. I made a mental note to check them when I got back to the house.

"Let's walk down to where you saw the truck pull out."

"That's the Sawyers' driveway," I said and realized I'd been an idiot not to check on them and make sure they were all right.

We walked down the road on opposite sides, shining our flashlights on the shoulders of the pavement. There was a bit of litter, but nothing that seemed particularly new or interesting. When we got to the Sawyers' driveway, we checked around the entrance. Their house, like mine, was set far enough back from the paved road that only a glow from its lights could be seen.

We squeezed through a gap in their gate, easier for me than for Pete, and walked up to the house.

The lights were on and there were a car and truck parked close to the nicely kept mobile home. I'd met the Sawyers a few times—a nice older couple who'd retired up to Adams County from Fort Myers. I could hear the TV going in the living room. I knocked on the door and heard footsteps approach. The porch light came on and I could feel myself getting the once-over through the peephole. Finally the door opened.

"Can I help you?" asked a friendly gray-haired man with bright eyes and an infectious smile. Mr. Sawyer had been in some type of sales, but I couldn't remember what.

"Mr. Sawyer, I'm your neighbor, Larry Macklin."

"Of course, I remember you, Deputy Macklin."

"This is my friend, Deputy Pete Henley."

"Right, right come on in."

"Who is it?" a woman shouted from the back of the house.

"Our neighbor," he yelled back to her. "Bring a couple cups of coffee."

"No, I'm fine," I said.

"I'll take one, thanks," Pete piped up. I gave him a dirty look. We were just there to check on the Sawyers, not to settle in for a neighborly visit. Pete just shrugged.

"Come on in here. We can sit at the dining room table." Mr. Sawyer guided us into the dining room and indicated two chairs. Reluctantly, I sat.

"We really don't want to take up your time."

"I figured this wasn't a social call," Mr. Sawyer said. "Some kind of trouble?"

"Did you see anyone hanging around your gate this

evening?" I asked.

He seemed to think hard about this. "Well, I just got home about half an hour ago." He thought some more. "I didn't see anyone, but I thought the area out in front of my gate looked a bit tore up. I figured it was those kids with the four wheelers. They ride down the right-a-way and a couple times it's looked like they've been doing wheelies or something in my drive."

"You know, I told you I thought you'd come home early," Mrs. Sawyer said, bringing in the coffee. "From the living room I can see the glow of headlights when someone turns into our drive, and I saw them about forty-five minutes ago and thought Fred was home."

"That's right, you asked what took me so long down at the gate."

"But you never listen to me," she kidded him.

"Guilty," he said, winking at her. Then he turned back to us. "Who was it?"

"I think someone's stalking me. I've had a couple of problems at my place lately." I saw the concern on their faces and rushed to reassure them. "I don't think these people are anything for you to be worried about. Just be extra vigilant for the next week or so." I took out a couple of my cards and gave one to each of them. "Call me anytime if you see or hear something out of the ordinary. If you see a stranger at your gate or at your door, don't approach them or let them in. Just give me a call. If you can't get me, call 911 and tell them that I told you to call."

They both nodded solemnly. "I've got a gun," Fred Sawyer blurted out.

"Don't even think about it, Fred," his wife scolded him. He pursed his lips, but didn't say anything else.

"Try not to confront anyone," I said to both of them. "Seriously, just call me. At night I'll be just down the road and across the street." They nodded some more and I looked over at Pete.

"The coffee is very good," he said to Mrs. Sawyer, who

then went off on a five-minute explanation of how to brew a great cup of coffee. She poured Pete a cup to go, then we finally headed out the door back to my place.

"Why didn't you call Darlene?" Pete asked suddenly, after we'd managed to squeeze through the Sawyers' gate again.

Taken by surprise, I had to think for a minute. "I didn't know if she'd have any game cams," I said reasonably.

"Bull. Did you even consider calling her?"

"If it was too late to call you at your house, I'm sorry," I said, a little irritated at the turn of the conversation.

"That's not the point. She's your partner," he stated flatly. Luckily, Pete couldn't see me roll my eyes.

"And you're my friend." I hoped this would end the conversation.

"Again, not the point. Look, I really appreciate the fact that your father still pairs up investigators," Pete said. "He could just randomly put investigators together when a case requires more manpower."

"I've heard his lecture. If we're used to working with someone, then we won't waste time when we have to team up. Okay, I get it. You think I need to work on my relationship with Darlene. That's easy for you to say." I was really not in the mood for this.

"Just sayin'."

"Maybe she and I just aren't a good fit. Maybe Dad screwed up putting us together." We had reached Pete's car now and I was getting more annoyed by the second.

"Bullshit. More likely you're just pissed off at yourself and at your dad, so now you're taking it out on Darlene," he said.

"Did she complain to you?" I asked loudly, letting my frustration with the entire situation boil to the top.

"I can see you aren't in the mood to talk." Pete opened his door and squeezed himself behind the wheel. "To answer your question, no, she didn't. But everybody at the office can see you're acting like an ass." With those words he put his coffee in a cup holder and closed his door.

He drove off, leaving me staring at his taillights. Grumbling to myself, I headed up the driveway to my house. *The boxes*, I remembered and went straight to my car.

Once I had all five of the boxes sitting on my living room floor, I started to open them and found myself sorting through memories. There were pictures, college textbooks, old receipts and other miscellaneous bits of a life that seemed very distant. I found a picture taken at my high school graduation. My parents were standing on either side of me. I felt a strong tug at my heart seeing Mom. Her smile was bright and pure, without any foreshadowing of the aneurysm that would take her life just two years later. Dad was smiling too, but his eyes were looking past whoever was holding the camera. *What was he looking at?* I wondered. With his arm around my shoulder, his coat was hitched up and you could see his old Smith and Wesson revolver and his gold badge. Dad was always on duty.

Ivy came over and helped me open the next box. This one was filled with clothes. I made sure there wasn't anything else in there, then gave it over to Ivy to play in.

The next one held old bank records and magazines. I started to push it away, then noticed that there was also a small cosmetics bag, a pair of women's tennis shoes and a book. I opened the bag, but there wasn't much in it other than dried mascara and a tube of lipstick that had oozed out all over the bag.

Picking up the book, I turned it over in my hands, trying to remember if it was one of mine or one that had belonged to Marcy. It was an ancient copy of *Treasure Island* and appeared to be a special edition prepared for schools. The back cover indicated it was printed by Southern Educational Publishers.

Everything else in the boxes was simply junk. I picked up the book and was going to sit down and thumb through it when my phone informed me that I'd received a text. It read: *Too much to text or tell you over the phone. Can you meet me at our usual place in 30 min?* It was Eddie. I wanted to tell him to go jump off a cliff, but I needed information on Marcy's motives now more than ever, so I said okay.

I looked at the book again. Something told me that I didn't want to just leave it sitting around in plain view so I took it to my gun safe and stashed the book inside before I left the house.

I drove to Rose Hill Cemetery. We'd started meeting there months earlier so that Eddie's family wouldn't know he was working with the sheriff's department. The Thompsons were deep into the drug trade and a number of other marginal or downright illegal businesses. Eddie held a strong grudge against most of them for their less than accepting attitude regarding his lifestyle choices. They didn't have a problem with him doing drugs, but they drew the line at him wearing women's clothes. Having a proclivity for abuse, Eddie's father was particularly cruel to him. Eddie got his revenge by supplying me with leads. A couple of months ago our department, with some assistance from the DEA, had put a serious dent in the family's operation and indicted several family members, including Eddie's father. Eddie had decided to take an extended vacation in Miami, but now he was back.

He was standing by an iron-fenced family plot at the back of the cemetery, smoking a cigarette, when I drove up. The air was cold and windy as I walked over to him.

"Good to see you, man," Eddie started.

"Cut the crap, Eddie. What's going on with Marcy?"

"She said you still had a thing for her."

"You have got to be kidding me. That statement just goes to prove how delusional she is. Do you know she broke into my house the other night?"

"Oh, yeah," Eddie said, as though he was proud of his vast knowledge of events.

"I'm not even going to ask if you knew about it ahead of time, because if you said 'oh, yeah', I'd have to beat the crap out of you."

"Hey, man, you can't do that."

"Sure I can. I'm pretty sure that's part of the CI contract. Don't you ever watch TV?" He stared at me, trying to determine if I was joking or not. "Eddie, the drugs are eating your brain."

"You got that right. I spent a lot of time messed up in Miami. Fun as hell, but might not have been too good for my sobriety."

I rolled my eyes. The jerk had a way of always making me feel sorry for him. Maybe I just felt bad that someone could make as many bad decisions as he had. The remarkable thing was that, once in a blue moon, he did something right. He'd managed to pass on information as well as saving my life twice now. So I took a deep breath and started over.

"I need to know what kind of craziness Marcy is up to. She's doing things that are going to get her, and those she's hanging out with, in trouble. The latter includes you," I told him in a fatherly way.

He looked down at the ground and did his best "aw, shucks" routine. "I know. She was bartending on South Beach. We hung out a little and then she got the word about her father." He shrugged and tossed his cigarette on the ground.

He started to speak again, but I stopped him. "Pick that up." I pointed at the cigarette butt.

"What?"

"Show some respect. Do you want to be haunted by one of these guys?" I asked, waving my arms at the tombstones. Right on cue, a gust of cold wind whipped past us. Grudgingly, Eddie picked up the cigarette butt, but then looked confused about what to do with it. Finally, he wet his fingers, put it out and stuck it in the pocket of his hoodie.

"Okay, I know about her father. Go on," I prompted.

"Yeah, anyway, so I was not doing well down there. Like, strung out every night, so I asked her if I could hitch a ride back home."

"When was this?"

"About two weeks ago."

"And you didn't bother to tell me you were back in town?" I was more than a little miffed.

"I was lying low, man. Once I got back, I started thinking about some of the guys that might want to hurt me. You know, after all that stuff…" He let that hang in the air. I actually *was* amazed that he'd been able to keep that low of a profile. "I went to some NA meetings and cleaned up. I'm clean. Really," he protested.

"Enough of the diary of a drug addict. I'm interested in what Marcy is up to."

"You are a lot more hostile than when I left," Eddie said, which almost caused me to throttle him. Maybe that proved his point. "Marcy's found out something that's got her all worked up. She's been acting really weird."

I took a deep breath. "What did she find out?"

"I'm not sure. She's gotten all secret squirrel about everything. I wanted a ride yesterday, and she was all, like, can't, you gotta walk, I'm not your personal chauffeur, blah, blah, blah. I saw her with a couple of guys a week ago, and when I asked what they were up to, she didn't want to tell me."

"What did these men look like?"

"One of them was short and pudgy. The other guy was tall, not fat, not too skinny. Middle-aged. The pudgy one looked a bit older. Not Marcy's kind of guys at all. She goes for the young party guys."

He didn't have to tell me. I'd always wondered what she'd ever seen in me. Looking back, I was probably her one attempt to have a real relationship. She wasn't very good at it.

"How did they act?"

"The guys were upset, and she was angry. Marcy kept looking back at me like she was afraid I might hear what they were saying."

"Where did this happen?"

"We'd pulled up to her house. Her parent's house, really.

She's staying with them. We were going to go drinking in Tallahassee and she needed money. When she got out of the car, the two guys came out of some place. I didn't see them."

I thought of my ambusher. Was this their MO?

"When she saw them, she told me to stay in the car. They went down by the street and talked."

"Did you get a look at their faces?"

"No, I was sitting in the car. I had to look over my shoulder to see them at all. Besides, it was already dark."

"Did you see their car?"

"No. Marcy came back to the car and said she had some money. We drove off. I didn't see where the two guys went." So they gave her money. Interesting.

"But she told you she broke into my place?"

"Said she needed to get something of hers. Not like she was stealing," he said, and I wondered what she would have called taking the money.

"Marcy didn't say what she was looking for?"

"She was just pissed that she couldn't find it."

"Okay, this is important. Like life and death important for you. Do I have your attention?" He looked a bit surprised and started patting his pockets nervously, looking for his pack of cigarettes. "Did she ask any questions about me, and did you answer or tell her anything about me?" I asked, thinking about Cara.

He squirmed and took out his cigarettes. "Maybe."

"Like where I live?"

"Maybe. Yeah." He took out his lighter. I reached out and took it away from him.

"Think. What else did you tell her?"

"I don't know. Not much. But it's a long drive up from Miami. I didn't tell her I was working for you or anything."

"Did she ask about my relationships?"

"They sort of came up. I said you had a girlfriend, but I don't even know who she is."

Eddie's attention span was wandering. I wasn't going to get much more out of him. I pulled out a twenty-dollar bill.

"This is a down payment. I want to know who Marcy is hanging with. Use your phone to take pictures. Find out what she's doing and let me know. Got it?" I held out the twenty.

Eddie looked at the money for just a second before taking the bill and stuffing it in his pocket. "I got it."

I turned and left him standing among the graves while I wondered how long he would be able to keep himself above ground. He was certainly living a high-risk lifestyle.

My phone rang before I was halfway back home.

"You might want to see what's burning at the sandpit," Darlene said. "I think we found the pickup truck."

CHAPTER EIGHT

The county-owned property known as the sandpit was a hundred acres used primarily as a source of sand for various construction projects. The county even made a little money selling sand from the pit to contractors.

The property was located at the south end of the county in the middle of pine woods that were owned by various timber companies. A chain-link fence and gate along the main road stopped any causal attempts to enter the area, but there were a dozen dirt trails and logging roads leading into it from other directions. The area was a favorite place for anyone wanting to sight-in their rifle. Both the sheriff's office and the county attorney had warned the commission that this was a liability nightmare, but every time the issue came up the commission looked at the cost to secure the pit and decided they'd rather ignore the problem. Even when we found a body on the property a couple of years ago, once they found out that the person had died from an overdose, they continued with business as usual.

I saw the glow of the fire as soon as I turned off the main road. I pulled through the gate and down to the edge of the pit. I could see a small tanker truck from the volunteer fire department sitting about forty feet back from the fire. A couple of firemen were standing around watching the flames while one guy held a hose and occasionally sprayed the burning truck. The truck's cab was blazing, but the fire was well past its peak.

A patrol car was parked near the fire truck. I saw a female deputy leaning against it with her arms crossed, watching the last of the fire. She looked over and I was a bit shocked to realize that it was Darlene. I got out of my car and she headed over to me.

"I've been keeping them from just dousing the truck with water, trying to preserve any evidence from the areas of the truck that weren't on fire. Did let them spray around where the VIN plates are."

"Good." She was right. If you let the firefighters have their way, they would empty the tank on the truck, washing away any evidence that didn't burn. "What are you doing in uniform?" I couldn't help but ask.

"I asked Lt. Johnson if I could do some patrol time. I've got to pay my dues like everyone else. I know everybody, but this gives me a chance to work with them in the same uniform," she said matter-of-factly.

This, combined with Pete's lecture, was making me feel guilty that I wasn't giving our partnership a chance. "Good thing you were working," I said, holding out an olive branch.

"I heard the call and was on this end of the county. Of course, when the call went out I had no idea it might be our truck. We still can't be sure. When I saw it could be ours, I asked dispatch who had called it in. According to them, a guy who does long-haul trucking and lives out on Pine Top Road saw the glow when he was on his way home. He called it in as a bonfire at the sandpit."

"I've got something I need to tell you," I started.

After I'd filled her in about the ambush that had taken place at my gate, she gave me a hard look, the fire reflecting in her eyes. "You should have called it in," she said flatly.

"You're right. But there are a lot of white pickups in the county, and I've had some trouble with intruders at my place recently, so I wasn't positive it was related." I hated having to defend my actions, but I hated it even more when I suspected that I'd made the wrong decision.

"You said you and Pete found a spent shell casing. Probably ought to log it in with the Parrish case," she said without judgment.

A call came in over the radio that was strapped to Darlene's shoulder. After a little back and forth with dispatch, she turned to me. "Accident. If you have this, I'll head over there," she said, already moving to her car.

When the sun came up, I was sitting in my car staring at the burned-out hulk of the truck. The clouds were gone, but the temperature had dropped down to near freezing during the night. I got out and checked the VIN number. It was definitely the stolen truck, probably the one used to steal the backhoe and most likely the one driven by the man who shot at me. I got back in my car and turned on the heater, waiting for the crime scene techs to arrive.

By noon, Marcus had finished processing the truck and we were watching the driver hook it up to a tow truck. As it pulled away, I had the feeling that we had reached a lull in the investigation. That vehicle had been our one tie back to the bad guy. Now that he'd ditched it, we didn't have much to go on. Marcus had pulled a palm print from the tailgate and some other trace evidence, but we'd have to wait to see if that got any hits with the NCIC.

I hadn't gotten much sleep watching the smoldering truck, so I quit work at three and went home to a blessedly peaceful house—no break-ins and no shoot-outs at my gate.

I was awakened from a long nap by Cara's knock at the door. She came bearing the gift of food—barbecue from Deep Pit. The smell made my stomach growl. I contained my hunger long enough to give her a kiss before diving into the pulled pork sandwich. Once my inner carnivore was satisfied, we talked a bit about recent events.

"*Treasure Island.* That sounds auspicious," Cara said.

"What it seems is a very odd thing for Marcy to have. She was never the literate type."

"Can I see it?"

I got the book out of the safe and handed it to her. She turned it over in her hands, looking at the cover. It was fabric-covered cardboard featuring the image of Long John Silver with his foot on a treasure chest, a couple of fellow pirates flanking him. Only two colors, black and red, had been used to print the image on the light blue cloth.

"This one was printed in 1930," she said, flipping pages. "There's a name." Cara pointed to a juvenile-looking scrawl in pencil on the first page of the story. *George Pike.*

"Marcy's last name is Pike," I mused. "So this *is* hers."

"I don't see anything else except some kid's stuff scrawled in the margins here and there," Cara said as she thumbed through the rest of the pages. She closed the book and handed it to me. "Are you going to give it back?"

Her question made me think. I hadn't considered what I would do if it was Marcy's book. I knew I ought to return it immediately, but some niggling voice deep down inside was telling me not to move too fast.

"I will. But I may wait a day or two and think about it."

George Pike. There was something about that name. When it came to old news, I knew who to talk to. I made a mental note to visit Albert Griffin, the unofficial official Adams County historian.

I put the book back in the safe, then joined Cara in the living room, turning down the lights as I went.

"Play some of that hippy music for me," Cara told me, and I pulled up a mix we'd recently made of folk songs and mellow classic rock.

She snuggled close. "There's comfort food and then there's comfort music," she said, reaching up for a kiss before we turned to the more advanced moves.

My plan to visit Mr. Griffin was put on hold. I was walking from my car to the office Friday morning when Darlene came running out of the building. For a second I wondered if the building was on fire, but when she saw me she came straight to me.

"Joe Parrish's body has just been found in his driveway," she said, going past me toward my car. I unlocked the doors and followed her.

Joe Parrish lived on the Parrish property, about a mile from the main house, in a nice brick ranch-style home that looked about ten years old. Deputy Julio Ortiz, who had answered the call, had already taped off the driveway and most of the surrounding area by the time we got there.

"No doubt he's dead," Julio assured us. "A big concrete alligator is sitting on top of his head. Or, I should say, where his head used to be. It's just a pancake now." The more gruesome the crime scene, the more irreverent the first responders and investigators tended to be. I was convinced it was a psychological defense mechanism.

I looked up the driveway. The house was on a rise about a hundred yards away, surrounded by hay fields. A couple of old oak trees flanked the house. I could just make out something lying in the driveway next to a pickup truck. The garage door was partway down.

Ten minutes later Shantel and Marcus pulled up in the crime scene van. They filmed as we walked up the hill to the body. Julio had not been exaggerating. Joe was lying on his stomach, and sitting where his head should have been was a forty-pound concrete statue of Albert the Alligator, the University of Florida's mascot. A large pool of blood, brain matter and skull fragments surrounded it.

"Looks like the statue came from over here," Darlene said. She was pointing to an area beside the driveway and near the garage where there was a deep depression in the flowerbed.

"We aren't looking for a small guy." I stated the obvious. To use something that heavy to attack a man as big as Joe would require strength and height. "And I think we can eliminate suicide as a possibility."

"Death by football mascot. Now I've seen everything," Marcus said while filming the body.

"If the murderer wasn't wearing gloves, we should be able to get some good DNA off the gator," Shantel said. "That concrete would take off some skin."

"Which means we have to do a damn good job coordinating with the guys from Darzi's office when they get here," I said.

We were all staring at the ground, looking for any piece of evidence that might have been left behind. The scene looked depressingly clean, but then a clean scene was easier to work than a messy one. At least if we found something, it would probably be important.

"Looks like he was dressed for work. Came out of the garage, went to get in the truck and was ambushed," Darlene suggested.

There was that word again—ambush. But how did that attack in my driveway tie in to the two murders?

"Are we on the same page that the two Parrish murders are connected?" I asked. The deduction seemed obvious, but there were some arguments against that assumption.

"Likely. But the method is radically different. Location is different. Time of day similar. Victim is a member of the same family, which suggests that the family is being targeted. We should warn the rest of them as soon as possible to take precautions. Of course, the odds that a family member is involved just went up a couple fold as well," Darlene stated.

I couldn't help but think of Hank Junior. Had he been asleep in his apartment again? The maid hadn't been able to corroborate his alibi for the time of the first murder.

Two murders in the same family. Clearly we were missing some connection. The profit motive for the family was stronger now. What would the survivors be set to gain by this second death? It all depended on Joe's will to dictate where his share of the farm went.

"He's got an ex-wife and a child. We need to know where she was," I told Darlene.

"I checked her address after the first murder. They live in North Carolina. I'll make sure they were there." As usual, Darlene was on top of it.

"Hard to picture a woman doing that," I said, looking at the alligator.

"It would take an Amazon to kill with that thing. I'm not sure that I could lift it high enough to hit someone. Of course, he might have already been on the ground," Darlene said thoughtfully.

"The ex could have hired someone to kill him. Wouldn't be the first time." I wondered if my ex had hired someone to accost me at my gate.

"You're not lying," Darlene said, lifting her eyebrows. Then she moved in and took a closer look at a spot of blood that had reached Joe's truck. "Looking at the blood splatter, it's possible that he might have been hit with something else and knocked to the ground."

"I'll call over to FDLE. They have a blood splatter expert," Shantel said as she photographed the blood.

We heard a commotion at the end of the drive. Looking down to where I'd parked, I could see one of the sisters was giving Julio hell. "I'll go help him," I said and started back down the driveway.

Julio had convinced Marge to sit in her car. As I came over, he handed her a bottle of water. When she saw me she brushed the water aside, jumped out of the car and ran over to me.

"I've got to see him. Who is doing this to us?" Her eyes were wild. She kept reaching up and tugging at her hair, clearly on the edge.

"We've got to process the scene. You can't see him right now," I told her, thinking: *I doubt you'd want to see him.* As it was, we were probably going to have to do a DNA test to be sure that the body *was* Joe Parrish, especially if he didn't have fingerprints on file and if his teeth and jaw where too badly damaged to test against dental records. This was one ugly murder. The only good thing I could say about it was that the victim still had his skin on, unlike a body we'd found in a hot tub a couple of months ago.

Marge stared into the distance and I began to worry that she was going to go into shock. Then I saw a truck come down the road and park erratically in the driveway. Hank and Jane jumped out.

"Your brother and sister are here," I gently told Marge. She didn't seem to hear me. I made the mistake of stepping toward Hank and Jane, who were hurrying over to us. I had no sooner moved out from between Marge and the driveway when she made a run for it. I had to turn and race to catch up with her.

You have to be very careful chasing down someone that you don't want to tackle or take a chance of tearing off their clothes. Essentially, I had to run ahead of Marge and let her charge into me. I grabbed her in a bear hug, then eased her back down the drive.

Once Marge was sitting in her car again, I took the opportunity to observe Hank and Jane. Jane was comforting Marge, kneeling at the open car door and gently touching her arm while talking quietly. Hank, on the other hand, was pacing and staring off at the woods. He obviously didn't want to meet my eyes or look at the distant body of his brother.

I had the sinking feeling that I'd made a mistake in not pushing Joe. He had known something, and now he couldn't tell me what it was. And here I was looking at another man from the Parrish family who was troubled. I wasn't going to go as easy on this one. I went over to Hank and walked right into his personal space.

"Your brother knew something that he chose not to tell me. Now he's been murdered like your father. I want to know every secret that this family has," I said bluntly.

Hank tried, but couldn't hold my eyes. "I don't know what you're talking about. I'm a recovering addict. That's my big non-secret. What else do you want to know?" There was an edge to his voice.

"I want to know why your brother was visibly upset when I showed him the holes that were dug in the woods." I hadn't mentioned the holes during my previous interview with Hank, but I had a hunch that Joe would have told the others. Hank's lack of surprise seemed to confirm this.

"Have you been to our lawyer?" he asked.

Where the hell did that come from? "No," I told him.

"So you don't know what's in my father's will?" He clamped his lips tight and his eyes went back to the woods. I followed his gaze and realized that we were looking at the same woods where the holes were dug. They were on the other side of a three-hundred-acre hay field and across the road, but they were there.

"At this point, all I know about the will is what your family told us. Were you all lying?"

"No, everything we told you was true. But there are a few small extra provisions in the will. One of them is for me." He stopped. I was about to prod him when he continued, "Dad left me the woods that run along the railroad tracks."

"Including the spot where those holes were dug, and the place where the person who killed your father was standing?"

"Yes. All told, about thirty acres on both sides of the tracks."

"Why?"

Hank sighed. "Why? Good question. Dad and I had an interesting relationship. Some of that went back to his father. I don't know if you ever met Granddad, but a harder, tougher, meaner old coot never lived. The only work he thought was worth anything was the kind you did with calloused hands and a strong back. I don't think he would have cared if any of us went to college or not, as long as we knew how to farm and hunt. Mom and Dad were a lot more easygoing, but Dad also did whatever his father wanted, and his father didn't want any dreamers in the family."

Hank stopped for a moment to gather his thoughts, then went on. "I was cursed with an imagination. Something Dad and Joe didn't have much of. One day when I was twelve, my teacher wanted everyone in our class to do a presentation on a local legend." Hank stopped and his hands searched inside his pockets, finding a vaporizer. He took a couple of deep draws on it. His hands were shaking.

"Are those things really better for you?" I asked, trying to calm him down.

"Hell if I know, but I have to do something," he said with the vehemence of an addict struggling to hold onto sobriety. "Anyway, I asked around, trying to come up with a topic. Then my mother told me about the old train robbery and how people believed that there was gold buried in our woods." He was staring off at the distant trees again.

I remembered the story. "The legend of the Nazi gold. I was about the same age when I first heard about that. I remember reading an article in the *Adams County Times*."

"They used to repeat the article every year or so. I got real excited and did all my research and began to dream about finding the gold. Dad went along with most of my daydreaming and didn't give me too hard of a time. He even went down with me to the woods a couple of times while I swung an old metal detector I'd borrowed. But when Granddad found out, he was furious. Told Dad that he'd better beat that nonsense out of me. Now, Dad wasn't going to do that. Even if he'd been inclined, Mom wouldn't have allowed it. I went on hunting down in those woods for a few years, off and on.

"What I didn't know was the price that Dad was paying for allowing me to pursue the legend. One day, I guess Granddad had found out from one of the farmhands that I'd been down there digging, and he raked Dad over the coals. Dad came to me and told me never to go into those woods again. Period. I was fifteen at the time, and I told him that he shouldn't let Granddad boss him around. I got a little too close to the truth, I guess, and Dad hit me."

I knew how complex father-son relationships could be. While my own grandfather had had the occasional mean streak when drinking, for the most part he had been an affable sort who'd never let my dad doubt that he was loved. If he had governed with the iron fist that Old Man Parrish had, my life might have been much different.

"Anyway," Hank went on, "Dad and I hardly spoke for years after that. The sad thing is that we both knew as soon as the punch had landed that he regretted hitting me, but we couldn't get past that moment in time. I think that's what hammered down the wedge between my mom and Dad. She left him as soon as I turned eighteen and she never came back.

"Dad told me this last time I got sober that he should have told his father to go jump off a bridge. He thought that that was the moment things went wrong between us, and I think he was right. He said he wished he'd let me explore and use my imagination any way I wanted. Dad told me that he wanted to leave those woods to me as a peace offering."

Did the holes and the murders have something to do with the legend of the gold, or the feud between Hank and his father all those years ago? And for all the information that Hank had offered me, I could tell that he was still holding something back.

"Do you think these murders have anything to do with the past or with you inheriting that piece of property?"

"I don't know. I hope not." He turned and went back to his sisters.

I looked back up the hill at Darlene, who was working the crime scene with Marcus, Shantel and a couple of deputies who'd volunteered to come out and help. I needed to fill her in. I trudged back up the hill and had almost made it when my phone rang. I looked at the ID—Deputy Andy Martel.

"What's up?" I asked.

"Got a guy here. Had a burglary that turned into a home invasion and now he wants to talk to you." Martel was in his early twenties and had been with the department for a little over a year. Whenever I talked with him, I always felt like I was talking to a suspect rather than a colleague. He volunteered as little information as possible.

"What's his name?"

"Griffin."

"Albert Griffin?"

"Yeah."

"Is he okay?"

"Banged up a little but, other than that, okay."

I thought about asking if he'd cleared the house, but Martel wasn't stupid, just stingy with information. "Put him on."

"Deputy Macklin?"

"Hey, Mr. Griffin. You okay?"

"Thanks to Brutus. I'm a little shaken up, though. I… I'd like to talk with you if you have the time." He sounded fragile. I knew that the older a victim was, the harder it could be to bounce back from an assault.

"I'm tied up right now, but I'll be able to come by your place this afternoon. You should let Deputy Martel call an ambulance and get you checked out at the hospital."

"No, no. I'm fine. Just fell down. I'll be waiting to hear from you."

"I'll be there as soon as I can," I said as I heard him hand the phone back to Martel. "Make sure that he's really okay, and get the house secured. How did they get in?" I asked him.

"Jimmied the back door. Old door, old lock."

"Do me a favor and make sure it's secure before you leave."

"10-4," Martel affirmed. As laconic as he was, he was a very conscientious officer.

CHAPTER NINE

I hung up the phone. Marge was still sitting in her car, staring at nothing. Jane and Hank were about ten feet from the car, talking too softly for anyone to hear them. Their faces were taunt and both of them looked ready to break out into an argument. Though why wouldn't they be tense and emotionally vulnerable? Their father and brother had both been killed in a matter of days. Was all of this about the family? I knew that an outsider was involved at some level due to the stolen backhoe, but they could have been brought into the murders by a family member.

I walked over to Darlene, who was poking around the front yard, bent over and staring at the ground.

"I don't really think there's anything to find here. Looks like the killer stayed on the driveway," she said without looking up.

"I didn't see any defensive wounds on the arms or hands," I said, "so he probably knew the killer."

"Big man like that," Darlene nodded over to where two of Dr. Darzi's people were trying to figure out how best to remove the concrete statue without further damaging the victim's body, "probably wasn't afraid of much. He might have let his guard down around a stranger."

Darlene brushed some leaves aside with her shiny shoes. Even when she wasn't wearing a uniform it still looked like she was, in her green polo shirt with the sheriff's office logo, khaki slacks and black polished shoes.

We spent another hour at the scene, even though there really wasn't much to see. Inside the garage and the house, everything looked in order. We walked Marge, Hank and Jane through the grounds to see if they could spot anything out of the ordinary. Nothing. Just to be safe, we had our IT guy come over and wrap up all of the electronics in the house for forensic analysis.

I thought about everything that Pete had said about bonding with Darlene. Even though I really wanted to have lunch with Cara or Pete, I suggested to Darlene that we stop at the Deep Pit Bar-b-que for my third helping of their artery-clogging food in as many days.

With pulled pork sandwich baskets in hand, we found benches inside the restaurant near the stuffed deer.

"You're from Tampa?" I asked as an opener.

Darlene looked up at me, setting her sandwich down and wiping her hands.

"I was raised there, but I was born in Missouri. My dad was a contactor and we moved to Tampa when the housing market was just starting to go crazy. Mom is a CPA." She looked at me, then said, "You always call me Darlene. Not Darl."

She'd made it a statement rather than a question, but I felt compelled to explain. "Darl is… kind of an ugly name," I said carefully, wondering if being honest and open with her was going to turn out to be a mistake.

She laughed. "That's the point. After having half a dozen guys call me Darling instead of Darlene, I knew I needed a gruff nickname to survive the world of cops. What's in a name? Funny thing is, the new nickname made a difference. All the grab-assers decided I must be butch with a name like that." She smiled. "Which I'm not. I'm just having a boyfriend dry spell at the moment."

"I guess fitting in *would* be a bit rough," I said, having seen some guys who couldn't stand the level of testosterone that pervaded most law enforcement ready rooms.

"I had a leg up. I worked with my dad on construction sites for a couple of summers. Same thing. Only difference is hammers instead of guns," she said. "So, do you like working for your dad?"

"Some days more than others," was the glib answer I gave her and then thought better of it. "At first, no. I was too much in his shadow. I joined the department for him." I paused. "Maybe that's not entirely true. It might also have been because I needed to prove that I was an adult. I guess when I thought about what an adult was like, I thought of my dad."

"You could do worse. From what I've seen, he's a straight shooter."

"Coming from Tampa, how'd you end up working for the Calhoun police?"

"I went to the Pat Thomas Law Enforcement Academy and Chief Maxwell was one of the recruiters that came and talked to our class. I guess I was pretty nostalgic for the small town in Missouri where we'd lived before coming to Florida. Also, Chief Maxwell has some pretty progressive ideas about law enforcement, so it seemed like the best of both worlds." Darlene almost sounded wistful.

"Why'd you change jobs?"

"Bigger department. Besides, Maxwell might become sheriff," she said with a mischievous smile.

Charles Maxwell was running against my father in the upcoming November election, giving Dad his first real challenge since he'd become sheriff. "Not if Dad has anything to do with it," I shot back, but kept my tone light.

"I'm good either way," Darlene said, picking up the last potato strip in her basket and eating it. "Best to stay out of politics."

"So why have you been razzing me with the rookie thing?" I asked. She'd started in with the rookie nickname the second day we'd worked together and, for some reason, it rankled me more than it should have.

"Because you don't take your job seriously," she said bluntly.

I felt the hairs on the back of my neck go up and my eyes narrow. "That's ridiculous." I had to work to keep my voice down. I wondered if I'd made a big mistake trying to get on friendlier terms with Darlene.

"Don't bow up at me. You asked. For one, look at the way you dress," she said.

What the hell? "What are you talking about? What's wrong with what I'm wearing?" I had on a button-down shirt and khaki slacks and didn't know where she was getting off criticizing my fashion sense. I felt the blood rising in my cheeks.

Darlene sat back in the booth and looked me straight in the face, her eyes dead serious. "The problem is you wear something different every day. Each day you come in and your holster is here or there. Your spare magazines are in a different spot on your belt. Sometimes your belt is leather, sometimes it's a web belt. The point is, if you have to draw your gun, you'd never know exactly where the butt of the gun is going to be. You take a chance of losing precious seconds getting it out of the holster and on target."

Now the blood was pounding in my ears. "How—" I bit back the *dare you.* "First shot off in a little over a second and a half, and on target. Anytime you want," I said through gritted teeth.

"Now you're getting all huffy." She rolled her eyes. "It's not just your tactical sense. What do you carry in the bag in your car?"

I wanted to end this conversation, but I couldn't find the right exit. "Stuff…" I spluttered. "Same as everyone else. I've got extra batteries, first aid equipment, trauma kit, extra magazines, a change of clothes and a bunch of other stuff." I couldn't believe her gall in challenging my law enforcement skills.

"I've never seen you take any of it out of your trunk," she said flatly. "In almost two weeks."

"What's that got to do with anything?"

"Do the batteries work? Are your extra magazines loaded? Has the ammo compressed the spring in the magazines? Would they feed correctly? Are any of the medical supplies out of date?"

"Just because you're Little Miss Girl Scout doesn't mean you're a good investigator." My response was churlish and silly, but the blood pounding in my head wasn't helping me come up with rational, snappy comebacks.

"I heard you didn't want to be a deputy, and what I've seen has just reinforced that idea. That's why I call you rookie. You remind me of a rookie who's joined up, but can't make the full commitment."

I counted to ten. If I hadn't, I would have said things that would have made working together damn near impossible. I think it was her righteous tone and attitude that irked me the most. I wanted to say something that would burn her the way that she was burning me.

"You don't like the way I do my job. I get it. I'll just say there are things that you do that I find irritating and we'll leave it at that." Sadly, that was the best I could do.

"You know what? If you think this is some personal bullcrap that I'm throwing at you, then you haven't understood a word I've said. So fine, forget it."

Now she's pissed at me? I thought. I suddenly noticed our waitress standing beside the table. She was young and looked embarrassed to have walked in on an argument. "More tea?" she asked in small voice.

"No," I said, taking out a five and leaving it on the table as a tip.

I'd planned on bringing Darlene up to speed on the silly Nazi gold angle, but she'd gotten me so pissed off that I didn't want to talk about it. We didn't say another word to each other until we were in the car.

"I think we should look very closely at the family," I said

in clipped tones that I pretended were professional.

"I agree. With two murders in the same family, it's not a stretch to think that the murderer is close by. Family, friend or employee." Darlene sounded like we hadn't just had an argument.

"I'll call Hank and tell him to meet us up at the main house with his sisters."

"And I'll check in with Shantel and see if they've wrapped up at the scene," Darlene said, taking out her phone.

I reached for mine to call Hank and almost dropped it as I took it off of my belt. I thought about what she'd said about fumbling my draw, then shook the thought off in irritation.

CHAPTER TEN

An hour later we were standing in the living room of the Parrish house with the surviving members of the family, as well as Clive and Andrew.

"Three days ago we were in this room, and we were discussing the murder of your father. Today we're here to talk about the death of your brother. This is beginning to look like a game of *And Then There Were None*. So I suggest that you all come to terms with the fact that you need to be completely honest with us. The sooner we catch the killer, the safer you will all be," I told them.

"Is that a threat?" Jane asked.

"It's just fact."

"What it sounds like is an accusation that we've been lying to investigators," Andrew the lawyer stated.

"At this point, I don't know if anyone here has been lying or not. But from my experience, every family has secrets. We don't care about anything that doesn't directly impact this investigation. Now's the time to come clean and let us decide what's important and what isn't." I gave them my best hardcore law enforcement stare and, no matter what Darlene thought of me, she was backing me up with a look that should have made any sinners in the group ready to confess.

Darlene and I had agreed that this time we'd do the family interviews together. On Tuesday, it had seemed likely that none of them were involved, but now it was hard to imagine that someone in the family wasn't connected to the murders.

We chose Hank first, following him into the dining room and sitting across from him at the table. He was visibly twitching as Darlene and I arranged ourselves and put a small pocket recorder on the table. Turning the recorder on, I looked up and caught Hank's eyes.

"For the record, I need you to say your name and that you agree to this conversation being recorded," I said.

Hank's eyes darted left and right. "Do you have to record it?" And before I could answer he blurted out, "Am I under oath or something?" And, again, before I could answer, he held up his hand in the universal stop sign. "No, I don't mean that. I'm fine with you recording it. I just…" His voice trailed off.

"If you're okay with the recording, would you please state your name and say that you are?" I suggested.

"Yeah, yeah. I'm Hank Parrish Junior and I'm fine with being recorded. Should I have a lawyer? Andrew said that none of us should answer any questions without a lawyer present."

"We just want to clear up a few things. I know that you want to help us solve the murders of your father and brother, right?" I asked, not answering his question. Because if I was honest, I would have told him that, in a murder investigation, no one should ever answer questions from law enforcement or the judicial system without a lawyer present. Period. But it wasn't my job to give him legal advice. My job was to get information out of him, and the best way to do that was to keep lawyers out of it.

"Of course I want to help solve the murders. More of us could be in danger," he said, sounding concerned, or maybe paranoid was a better word.

"Until we get some answers, there is no way for us to

know how much danger the rest of the family is in," I said honestly.

"Where were you this morning?" Darlene shot at him. We'd agreed that she'd ask the direct questions, and I'd do more open-ended ones since he and I had bonded a bit at the scene.

"Again, like Tuesday, I was asleep at my place," he said, looking down at the table.

"Think hard. Can anyone verify that? 'Cause the maid didn't back you up last time."

"Some stupid wrong number woke me up. The sun wasn't up yet, but there was light coming in the window."

"Can I see your phone?" Darlene asked, putting out her hand. He looked at her hand for a minute before reaching into his pocket and pulling out his phone. He swiped at the screen and put the phone in her hand.

"Just after seven," Darlene said. "The call lasted thirty seconds. The caller ID is unknown."

"Yeah, it was someone looking for someone else. Like they were supposed to pick them up or something," Hank said rather vaguely.

Cell tower pings wouldn't help in this case. Hank's bedroom wasn't that far from where his brother was killed. Both locations would use the same cell tower. An unknown number could indicate anyone with a burner phone, but thirty seconds seemed a little long for a wrong number.

"Did either of your sisters have anything against Joe? Do you know of any hard feelings between them?" I asked, partly to distract Hank so that Darlene could spend a little extra time scanning through his phone.

"No, I don't think so. Until I got sober, I hadn't had much to do with the family lately, so something could have happened between them," he said softly.

Interesting, I thought. Not so much that he thought there was a possibility of hard feelings, but that he left that door open. Was it to divert suspicion from himself?

"Can I have my phone back?" he asked Darlene, who

grudgingly handed the phone over to him.

"Who benefits?" Darlene asked flatly.

"What do you mean?" Hank sounded evasive.

"She's asking who will benefit from your brother's death. Financially or otherwise," I answered.

"I guess all of us. My sisters and me." He'd done it again, not trying to defend Marge or Jane at all.

"What about Joe's daughter?"

"Oh, um, I heard that her mother married some rich guy and she doesn't need the money. Joe thought that if he left any money to his daughter that her mother would get it and he hated her. Really hated her." Hank was rambling. Was it guilt?

"Who told you about Joe's will?"

Hank hesitated for a moment. "Jane. You know she's a paralegal. Joe talked to her about it a couple of years ago when Dad had to go to the hospital for some tests."

"How much money are we talking about?" Darlene pushed.

"Hell, I don't know. Do I look like someone who knows anything about money?" His emotions were running the gambit of frustration, fear and anger.

"You must have some idea," I said.

"A lot, I guess, but Dad complained all the time about his overhead. The cost of diesel, keeping the tractors and bailers working, and the laborers. I understand enough to know that without Dad and Joe, this place is probably going to go belly-up." Now there was just sadness and self pity in his voice.

I thought about asking him if he might try to run the place, but it would have been a stupid question. Anyone could see that he wasn't capable—mentally or emotionally.

"You think you all will just cash out?" Darlene suggested, trying to keep him on the topic of money. With some suspects, if you got them talking about something that excited them, then they just couldn't seem to control what came out of their mouths.

"Who knows? I imagine that Marge will get her back up and nothing will happen for years. Jane… She'd sell… I think."

"You don't think they'll agree on what to do?"

"Those two? They haven't agreed on anything for decades. Marge will want to run the farm and Jane will want to cash out as soon as possible." Hank put his face in his hands.

"Jane wants the money?" I asked.

"Hell, I don't know. I didn't say that. She certainly never cared for the farm. But I don't want to talk about them. If you want to know what they're thinking, you'll have to ask them. And as far as who might have killed Joe, I can't imagine. He could be an ass, but mostly to me." Hank started to cry.

We watched him for a minute before he wiped his eyes and asked, "Can I go now?"

I looked over at Darlene. She nodded her head. I wanted to ask Hank some more questions about the holes at his father's crime scene and any possible connection to the gold legend, but since I hadn't filled Darlene in on that yet, I didn't want to bring it up right now.

"Sure, but we'll want to talk with you again," I told him.

Nodding and choking back tears, Hank got up and left.

I asked Marge to come in next. She had on her best Winston Churchill face—grim and determined.

"I'm sorry that you all have had to suffer these loses," I said and meant it.

"And I'm sorry that we have to ask you these questions. But they are necessary if we're to find the murderer, or murderers, that are preying on your family," Darlene told her.

"Murderers? Could there be more than one?" Marge asked, her eyes wide.

"We have to look into to all the possibilities," I said.

"Of course. But I'm finding it hard to come to terms with one monster on the loose, let alone two or more." She shook her head as though to clear it of such a disturbing thought.

"Can you tell us where you were this morning?"

"At school, the same as Tuesday."

We went through the timeline of when she arrived and who saw her. "And before I went to school, Clive and I had breakfast together."

"What about Clive? What did he do after you left for school?" I asked.

"I don't know exactly. You'd have to ask him. But he usually goes to work in the office. His office is in our home," she explained.

"What does he do?" I asked.

"Honestly, I don't really understand what he does. He does consulting work for companies all over the world, designing something to do with computer networks and how they talk to each other. I learned a long time ago not to ask him about his work." This last comment almost made her smile.

"You all live in Leon County?"

"Just over the line. We both worked in Tallahassee when we got married, so it was nice not having too long of a commute. Plus, I was only twenty minutes from Mom and Daddy."

"Your mom and dad were divorced?"

"Yes, and then Mom got sick. Cancer." Marge started to cry and we gave her a few minutes to compose herself. Drying her eyes with a tissue from her pocket, she went on, "Just everyone is gone."

"Why did your parents break up?" Darlene asked her.

"How could that have anything to do with... this?" Marge asked.

"At this point, we don't know what's important and what isn't."

"Okay, in my opinion, the cause of the trouble between them was always my grandfather. He rode Daddy hard. Heck, he rode everyone hard. Mom included. She tried to get

Daddy to put his foot down, but that wasn't going to happen and eventually she just disconnected. She waited to leave until all of us kids were out of high school, but she'd given up long before that." Marge's face reflected all of the pain of the last few days. "Honestly, I blamed all the years of stress for her cancer."

"I know we asked you this before, but can you think of anyone that would have a grudge against your family?" I asked.

"No," she said after a pause.

"I'm sorry that I have to ask this next question, but you need to realize that we are looking at every possibility, no matter how unlikely. With your father and brother dead, who will inherit most of the property?"

Marge's eyes got hard and cold as she looked from me to Darlene. "You can't honestly be suggesting that one of us killed them," she stated. "That's insane."

"We have to look at a profit motive in any murder. We just have to. We're going to dig till we find out the truth, so there's no reason for you to not answer the question." Darlene returned Marge's cold, hard look.

"I don't have to talk to you at all," Marge said as the farm woman in her came out. "Jane and Andrew said that you all would come after us."

"Marge, we aren't accusing anyone of anything," I said, trying to reason with her. "You know that if you're working on a hard problem, sometimes that best way of approaching it is to eliminate the extraneous solutions. That's what we're trying to do here. Nothing would make me happier than to be able to take all the members of your family off of the suspect list."

Marge pursed her lips and narrowed her eyes as she thought about my argument.

"I'm really not sure how it will work out. I'm not a lawyer. Most of the inheritance from Dad was to go into a trust. I haven't seen the will for years. I guess that Joe's share will be split between us, or it might go to his daughter, Ellie.

We haven't seen her in years. Joe and his ex-wife had a very nasty divorce." Marge put her hand over her mouth. "I hadn't even thought. I don't know if anyone has told them. Poor Ellie." Tears came down Marge's cheeks again.

I made a note to check in with Joe's ex and check her alibi, though North Carolina is a long way from Florida. And if her daughter wasn't going to inherit, then what motive would she have? These murders just seemed to be spreading misery over a larger and larger area.

After a few more routine questions, we ushered Marge out. She said that she'd find a number for Joe's ex, inform her of his death and get us the number.

Jane came in next with her boyfriend, Andrew.

"We would really like to talk to Jane alone," I told him.

"That's not going to happen," Andrew said, with an attitude somewhere between protective boyfriend and jerk lawyer.

I turned to Jane. "I know you want to find the person or persons responsible for these murders. The best way for this investigation to proceed is for us to talk with each of you separately. We don't think that either of you had anything to do with these murders, but we just need to gather the facts so we can move forward with the investigation." Actually, we had no idea whether they were involved or not, but lying to suspects is permissible and, sometimes, even desirable.

"Can you honestly say that Jane is not a suspect?" Andrew asked snidely. From the last set of interviews, I knew that he was a real estate lawyer and not a criminal lawyer. He probably had just enough knowledge of the legal system, backed up by zero experience, to hang himself and Jane if they were guilty.

"You know we can't eliminate anyone. Not even you," I told him.

"I would like Andrew to be here as my friend, if not my lawyer," Jane said. She seemed contrite enough, but I couldn't tell if it was an act or if she really was coming to the interview as an open book.

Darlene and I looked at each other and we both nodded. "Okay, but I would like you to let Jane answer our questions without interruption," I told Andrew. He raised his hands and put on a *whatever you want* expression that I didn't believe for a minute.

They sat down next to each other across the table from Darlene and me.

"Jane, where were you this morning?" Darlene asked, pen poised above her notepad.

"At my place in Tallahassee." We knew that Jane lived on the west side of Tallahassee, closest to Adams County. This fact made a difference. The Tallahassee system of roads was clearly created without any plan in mind, and because of this it could take anywhere from thirty minutes to an hour to get to Adams County, depending on where in Tallahassee you lived.

"What time did you learn that your brother had been killed?" Darlene asked in a business-like manner.

"Marge called me as soon as she learned what happened. I guess it was about eight-thirty."

"Eight-forty-five," Andrew piped in, pulling up the call on Jane's cell phone.

"Mr. Simmons, please don't interrupt," I said, trying to freeze him with my stare. He seemed unfazed, but shut up.

"And you were at home until that time?"

"Yes, I was. Andrew had left for work, but I'd taken today off. I was going to come over here and help Joe and Marge get ready for Dad's funeral." Interesting that she didn't mention Hank Junior. His black sheep status was well established.

"Can you think of anyone who might have wanted to hurt your brother?" As she asked the question, Darlene locked eyes with Jane.

"No... not really," Jane said, clearly begging us to ask who she was thinking of.

"You sound like you have someone in mind," I said flatly.

"I… don't want to say."

"You don't have to answer," Andrew said and we all ignored him.

"Other people could be in danger. Anything you say is simply one piece of the puzzle. If there is someone that had a beef with your brother, tell us, and the odds are we'll be able to clear them quickly if they had nothing to do with the murder," I said, trying to persuade her. Andrew snorted in derision.

"I can't say anything," she said. Andrew started to pipe up and I put up my hand to stop him.

"Think carefully about this, Jane. Not taking action has its own set of consequences. I know you don't want there to be another tragedy, one that you could have prevented," I pleaded. I wasn't sure that this wasn't all an act, but I wanted to give her the benefit of the doubt.

Everyone was quiet as Jane pursed her lips. "I really don't know anything," she said. "But you do have a point. I saw my old boyfriend in Calhoun earlier this week. He was in a red car and some woman was driving."

"You mean Joel Patrick?"

"Yes."

"Why didn't you call us? You knew that we were interested in him," I asked, wondering if the woman in the red car could have been Marcy. Was Joel one of the men Eddie had seen her with?

"I just didn't take that seriously. The fight he had with Dad was soooo long ago. I didn't want to get him in trouble, but now with Joe's… passing."

She gave us the approximate time and place where she had seen Joel and we asked a few more routine questions before turning to Andrew. He refused to give us anything else.

Clive was the last person we questioned. He corroborated Marge's answers with an engineer's dreamy detachment. He claimed to have been around his wife's family, but not really *of* the family. He was pretty believable as a good guy who didn't really notice the hurly-burly of the real world.

"Hank's hiding something and Jane has something up her sleeve," Darlene said when we got back in the car.

"Agreed," I said, pondering what our next move should be. "I think we have to approach this from both angles. I still think that there is an outside influence involved here, but I'm equally convinced that there has to be a family angle to the murders."

"Makes sense. If we can figure out the purpose for that backhoe digging holes, I think we'll be a couple of steps closer to finding the killer," Darlene said.

"I've got a little insight into that," I told her as we got into the car. "I need to swing by and check on someone on the way back to the office. I'll fill you in on the way."

CHAPTER ELEVEN

As we drove to Albert Griffin's, I told her about the legend of the Nazi gold and Hank's connection to it.

"People seriously believe in that story?" she asked. "I've heard about it, but I wouldn't put any more faith in it than the lost Dutchman's mine or the money pit on Oak Island."

"I know. But you can't convince some people."

I thought that while we were checking on Mr. Griffin, we could ask him what information he had about the legend. I was looking forward to introducing Darlene to him. Pete had shown me what an asset the county historian could be when we were dealing with an investigation that had deep roots in the history of the community. Darlene might have had an edge with her technical police skills, but when it came to knowing the community, I figured I had the upper hand.

The sun was almost touching the tops of the trees as I knocked on the door. Mr. Griffin answered, looking worse for wear after his run-in with a burglar.

"Deputy Macklin. Thank you so much for coming by," he said, working hard to put on his trademark smile. A bandage covered a large bump on his forehead, just below his thinning gray hair. I turned to Darlene, planning to introduce them, when Mr. Griffin threw up his hands in glee.

"Darlene Marks! My word. I'd heard you were working for the sheriff's office now. We missed you at the last historical society meeting." He was beaming. Apparently, seeing my partner was such a delight that he forgot about the trauma he'd endured.

"I've just been so busy with the job change and all. I did hate to miss Tate's talk on north Florida railroad lines," Darlene answered with a smile. So much for my upper hand.

"You know, I thought he might be rather dull, but it turned out to be a very interesting presentation," Mr. Griffin said, then remembered me and why we were there. "I'm sorry. Come in," he said, backing away from the entrance.

"Tell us what happened," I said when we were standing in the living room which, like the rest of the house, was filled with bookcases and boxes of files and old newspapers.

"I think that it was really my fault," Mr. Griffin said, touching the bandage on his forehead.

"I don't see how being burglarized and hit on the head can be your fault," I offered.

"Oh, no. What I mean is that the fellow probably thought I was gone. Didn't realize that Nancy had brought me home," he said, which didn't clarify things very much.

"Why don't you start at the beginning?" I suggested.

"Of course, that's how things should be done." Mr. Griffin smiled at us. "Simple enough. My poor Volvo needed some work. I decided I'd take it up to Stan's Repairs. He told me that if I dropped it off this morning he'd look at it and order the parts. So I took it in, and Nancy—my neighbor, Nancy Odom—picked me up and drove me home."

"And you think the burglar got in and didn't know you'd come home?" Darlene said.

"Precisely. You see, I told Nancy to just park at her place and I'd walk home. Naturally, I came in the back way since Nancy parks behind her house. The shortest route is through the hedges to my back door. I imagine the fellow was keeping an eye on the front for me and never thought that I might come in the back."

"So you came in the back door. Why don't we go back there and retrace your steps?" I suggested.

"Good idea."

We followed him out into the main hall. The house was old and large but, with all of the books and records, it had a claustrophobic feel. I noticed a few of his rat-catching cats lurking about the stacks as we walked to the kitchen.

"I entered there," he said, pointing toward the cottage door. At some point in the house's history, the back porch had been converted into a kitchen. The original kitchen would have been located behind the house and accessed by way of a dog walk. In the days before air conditioning, and when cooking was a serious fire hazard, common sense dictated putting a little distance between the kitchen and the main house.

"When you came in, did you hear anything?" Darlene asked. She was looking around the room like a bloodhound trying to get a scent.

"No. Of course, I was pretty distracted, wondering how much the car repairs were going to cost. But I didn't notice anything out of the ordinary. I headed down the hall toward the stairs."

We followed him back down the hall until he stopped at the door to a room that I imagined was meant to be the dining room, but that now, like the rest of the house, more resembled a library with several rows of shelves forming stacks.

"It was when I was passing here that I heard some papers fall. I turned and there he was," Mr. Griffin said with amazement, as if he was seeing the man appear before him as he spoke. "I turned and said, 'What the devil?' and he looked at me. That's when he picked up the crowbar that was sitting on the shelf. He must have brought it with him. He came at me and I... Well, I hate to admit it, but I screamed." He paused and looked at both of us. "And do you know what happened then?" Mr. Griffin was enjoying the dramatic moment.

"What?" I asked, giving him the pleasure of an engaged audience.

"Brutus!" he said and, after a second, I remembered that Brutus was the name of a particularly burly black cat that stalked the house. "Brutus must have been watching from the top of one of the stacks, because when the man came at me, Brutus jumped down on top of him. The man cursed, flailed about and hit me as he ran past. I don't think Brutus let go of him until the man was at the front door."

Brutus appeared around one of the shelves as though conjured by the mention of his name. Darlene squatted down and held out her hand. The black bruiser came straight over to her and let her pet him. Did everyone like Darlene?

"What did the man look like?" I asked, trying to ignore the meeting of the mutual admiration club on the floor.

"He wasn't very tall. He had on a hoodie. White man, I think. Really didn't get a good look at his face. He had the hood pulled up and a scarf over half his face. I'd like to say I was totally calm, but that would be a lie. Especially when he picked up the crowbar. I can give you an excellent description of the crowbar if you want." He chuckled.

"What do you think he was after?"

"That's the funny thing. He was rooting around in these old stacks instead of looking for valuables. He didn't even go for my rare books. They're in the room across the hall." Mr. Griffin walked over to a shelf that seemed to be a bit jumbled compared to the careful order of the other stacks.

"The man was holding this." He picked up a large portfolio. "Just bound copies of the local paper from 1946." Albert held the book out to me.

The date sent chills down my spine. I had a growing suspicion that all of this was tied together.

"This may seem like an odd question, but would there have been any articles about the train robbery in these papers?"

"Train robbery?" He frowned, then his eyes widened and

his face was lit with a huge smile. "Yes, our own version of the Great Train Robbery, but much less successful. Of course, it wasn't a robbery at all. Come on, this way."

He took the book and we followed him back into the living room where he set it down on a coffee table. "Sit down. Would you like something to drink?" We both turned down the offer and took seats around the table.

Mr. Griffin carefully turned the pages of the old newspapers to the back of the book. "Here we are." He tapped a headline that read: "Three Dead on Army Train."

Darlene and I bent forward and read the article.

Adams County—Two local men are dead and one is missing following a scuffle on an Army train passing through our county. In addition, another soldier was killed. According to the Army, a fight broke out when the three local boys, identified as George Pike, Phillip Thompson and James Patrick, attempted to jump from the train when it slowed down at a crossing near Parrish Farm. Sergeant Miles Cook attempted to stop the men and one of them hit him hard enough with a metal bar to fracture his skull. Another soldier, not identified, witnessed the attack on Cook and fired at the fleeing men. Thompson and Patrick were killed. The military is still looking for Pike. Cook later died in Tallahassee from his wound.

"No gold," I said, not surprised at all.

"No. The gold story came out a couple years later. Wait." Mr. Griffin flipped to the very last paper in the portfolio, dated two weeks later, and tapped the lead story: "Fugitive Captured!"

Adams County—On Wednesday the military captured George Pike. The fugitive, wounded during his escape, appeared to have been hiding at the Ol' Kettle off of Jefferson Street. According to Colonel Eckart, Pike will be transported to Camp Blanding where he will be tried by a military court and, if found guilty, will be incarcerated at Fort Leavenworth in Kansas.

The article went on to provide details about the capture of Pike, including the fact that a woman of questionable morals tipped off the authorities.

"Still no mention of any gold," Darlene said.

"From what I've been able to gather from my research, the legend of the gold originated with George Pike. The first mention was a letter that he wrote, or I should say scrawled, from Leavenworth to his brother," Mr. Griffin said. "I have a copy in my files."

"Pike made up the story about the gold?" I asked.

Mr. Griffin smiled. "Or the military made up the story that the men were just going AWOL." He let that sink in for a moment before continuing, "But, in my opinion, Pike made up the story so that he and his dead companions didn't look so stupid. I think that after serving in Europe—and I should say that they all did serve honorably in the war—they were tired of being in the Army and the temptation of riding a train through their own backyard was just too much. You have to remember that a lot of the servicemen were sick and tired of military life after the war ended. They felt like they'd done their duty and should be able to go home. There were actual protests in Europe and around the world in 1946 by troops that just wanted to come home and were unhappy with the speed at which the Army was demobilizing."

"So stealing gold sounded better than going AWOL?" I asked, a bit suspicious.

"He also used the story to get his friends here in Adams County to send him stuff. He was telling them that he hid the gold before he was captured, and hinted that anyone who helped him might get a share. He had been sentenced to twenty years for his part. All the witnesses agreed that it was Thompson who actually hit Cook, so the military court was lenient with Pike. But it didn't matter. The wound that Pike received never healed properly, and he died of complications. His official cause of death was pneumonia, but he was in Leavenworth's hospital being treated for an infection related to the old wound."

"That makes more sense, using the story to get help from his hometown buddies," Darlene said.

"One of his last letters even hinted at an escape attempt. Pike was trying to convince his brother to come out with some friends and break him out of jail. All ridiculous, of course. We're talking Leavenworth," Mr. Griffin said dismissively.

"I went through a period when I was a kid where I believed in the lost Nazi gold." I shook my head sadly.

"It could all be true and the government was just trying to cover up the fact that they were sneaking gold out of Europe after the war," Mr. Griffin said, not sounding like he believed it for a moment.

"Much more likely he was just using the story to get what he wanted." That's when it hit me. Pike. George Pike. The same name that was in Marcy's book. Sadly, manipulating people seemed to be a family trait. But it still didn't explain why Marcy wanted the old book so badly.

"And the same can be said about the *Adams County Times*. They rehashed the Nazi gold story every year and Stan, the editor in the nineties, told me it always tripled sales."

"I'd like to see whatever else you have on the legend," I told him.

He stood up quicker than you'd expect for a man his age. "Be right back," he said

"You really think this has something to do with our murders?" Darlene asked as we waited for Mr. Griffin to return.

"It's too big of a coincidence. That backhoe was stolen so that someone could dig holes on the Parrish land. Maybe they were looking for the gold and maybe Hank Senior just stumbled on the men trespassing and got shot for his trouble."

"And Joe?"

"Maybe he saw something. Or maybe someone is taking advantage of the first murder to eliminate Joe, thinking that it would be falsely linked to Hank's murder."

"That's a lot of maybes," Darlene pondered. Before she could say more, we heard Mr. Griffin shout from another room. We followed his voice and found him in the back corner of the room where he'd been assaulted.

"Look at this," he said, pointing to an open filing cabinet drawer. "Oh, of course, you can't see what's missing." He shook his head. "I had a file in here clearly marked 'Nazi Gold'. It's gone."

"How big was the file?" Darlene asked, and I knew where she was going with the question.

"Not too large."

"Could the man who attacked you have had it with him?" Darlene followed up.

Mr. Griffin closed his eyes tight and thought about the question. After a moment, he opened his eyes and nodded. "It's possible. The hoodie that he was wearing was large and baggy. He might have even had it stuffed in one of the hoodie's pockets. Like I said before, I was focused on that crowbar."

"Don't touch the cabinet. I'll be right back," Darlene said, heading out to the car for the fingerprint kit. She returned and dusted it quickly. Nothing. Not surprising. Mr. Griffin said he thought the man had been wearing gloves.

"So it *is* all about the gold," he mused.

"Looks like it," Darlene said.

We left him with some stern advice about upgrading his security. He assured us that he had plans in the works and that his nephew would be staying over every night until they had things fixed.

Exhausted, I pulled out of Mr. Griffin's driveway and headed back to the office so that Darlene could pick up her car.

"About earlier," I started. Emotionally and physically tired, I wanted to put the tension between Darlene and me to rest, so I waded back into deep waters. "I admire the fact that you take your job seriously. And if I'm being honest, it wasn't that long ago that I wasn't sure whether I even wanted to be a deputy. But a lot has happened over the last couple of months. I've stepped into some bad situations and haven't always made the right decisions, but I've learned that

I have something to contribute to the department. I'm determined to do my job and do it the best I can."

"And that's all I'm talking about. I could give you the standard line about how I'm a girl and so I had to work harder at my job, but that's not it. I'm this type of woman. I'm this kind of cop. I double check to see if my front door is locked. I empty out my magazines every other day and reload them. That's just who I am. I've got a lot of my dad in me."

I couldn't help laughing.

"What?" Darlene asked, puzzled.

"Nothing to do with you. I was just thinking about how many father issues I've had to deal with in the last few months. My own and others. Sorry. At least you got some usable traits from yours."

"Cops, crooks and construction workers. They're all mostly about testosterone. 'Sides, I'm happy with what I got from my father. Anything he built will be standing long after other buildings have crumbled into dust," she said proudly.

"What you said about that being the way you are. I think that's true about most people, me included. We are who we are. The best we can do is find where we fit in, and maybe work to polish off some of our rougher edges."

"I get that. And I promise you, if I didn't think you were an okay cop I would have already been in the sheriff's office fighting for a new partner," Darlene assured me.

We spent the rest of the drive in the most comfortable silence we'd shared as partners.

Before we parted at the office we agreed to a rough itinerary for Saturday. We still needed to interview all of the Parrishes' employees about the second murder, and I wanted to talk with some of their neighbors. We talked with dispatch and, as vague as it was, gave them a description of the man who burglarized Albert Griffin to put out on the radio as wanted for questioning in a homicide. We also issued a BOLO for Joel Patrick. Now that we knew he was in the area, I wanted to talk with him too.

I called Cara when I got home and we agreed that, baring more dead bodies, we would spend Sunday together. I had a special place in mind where I wanted to take her. I told her to dress for a hike, but otherwise kept mum regarding our destination. After feeding Ivy, checking my email and having a quick dinner, I crashed into bed and dreamed of Nazi gold.

CHAPTER TWELVE

Saturday went pretty much the way I'd expected it would—lots of talking met with blank faces and head shakes. We'd enlisted the help of a couple of patrol deputies to assist with canvassing the neighbors, but since, in this part of the county, a close neighbor was one that was less than a quarter of a mile away, no one saw or heard anything useful.

We were done by three and I headed home, where I found Cara waiting for me. She'd planned to stay overnight so we could get an early start in the morning and she'd brought Alvin along with her.

"Ivy, he's not going to bother you," I told the little tabby as she studied him with piercing eyes from the back of the sofa. Alvin was lying on the floor, making small snoring sounds with his back feet splayed out behind him.

"The funny thing is, I think he's fascinated with her," Cara said. We'd just finished dinner, delicious fried catfish that she'd picked up at the Missionary Church of Our Savior. The church was one of a dozen small congregations on the south side of town, and its membership included two elderly men whose life's work was fishing and the frying of that fish.

I looked at the Pug, whose eyes were shut tight as his small body moved up and down with his rhythmic breathing.

"I wouldn't call that fascinated, more like comatose," I said.

"You should have seen him in the car when we pulled up to the house."

"Your car smelled of the best fried fish in north Florida. Of course he was excited," I kidded her.

"Now you saw the way he was watching her earlier. Alvin's just worn out from following Ivy around," Cara said in a last-ditch effort to convince me that Alvin was obsessed with something other than his stomach.

"I wouldn't mind wearing myself out obsessing over someone I love," I said with arched eyebrows, which lead to a playful kiss and then on to other things.

The next morning we packed some snacks for us and for Alvin before heading to my car. The weather was chilly, but the sun was already peeking above the trees as we drove out through my gate.

We hadn't gone more than a mile when my phone rang. I looked at the number and frowned. It was Deputy Julio Ortiz, who'd done too many favors for me to be ignored.

"Hope I didn't wake you," he said.

"No, I'm up and moving. What's going on?"

"I was working last night and happened to drive by that piece of land by the railroad tracks where the first Parrish murder took place. I saw a car parked down the road a bit— off the road, but not in a place where someone would park a car unless they didn't want it to be noticed. You know what I mean? Anyway, I checked it out. No one was around. Maybe it just broke down or ran out of gas. I tagged it with a warning. But the best part... The registration matches that BOLO you issued last night for Joel Patrick."

My stomach dropped.

"I drove by the spot again this morning on my way off shift. The car was still there," Julio finished.

"Thanks, Julio, I'll check it out," I said and hung up. Joel Patrick, the one-time boyfriend of Jane Parrish, whose father had turned up dead not far from where Patrick's car was now parked. Not even a chance that this was a coincidence. And, for bonus points, Patrick had recently been seen riding in a red car that may or may not have been driven by my crazy ex.

"I really, really hate to do this, but I need to swing by and check on something," I said to Cara, meaning every single word.

"Sure, that's fine," she said. I appreciated the fact that there wasn't any irritation in her voice. "Does this have to do with the Parrish murders?"

"Possibly. There's a car that's parked near where the first murder took place. Julio said it's been there at least since last night and there's no one around." I didn't go into any details about suspects. As an investigator, you can't just go around giving out details about a case, even to people who you're close to and who aren't a part of the investigation. Leaks have a way of becoming rivers that can drown a person.

I had to back-track a bit to get to the Parrish property. Assuming that I could check the car out, and possibly have it towed, it shouldn't have been more than an hour before we were back on the road.

I found the car pretty easily. The older model Mazda hatchback didn't look like it had been cleaned in months. Peering through the cloudy windows, I could see that the back was filled with tools. I could make out drills, shovels and a ratty gray blanket covering what looked to be a metal detector. The doors were all locked. Julio had placed an abandoned car notice under the windshield wiper on the driver's side.

The clearing where the backhoe had been found was about a hundred feet back down the road. There was nothing where the car was parked except the small pull-off. There were a lot of similar places in the county where, in the fall, hunters parked their pickup trucks while they hunted for deer or turkey. The land in all directions was woods.

If Joel was out here, I was sure his motives centered on

the area where the holes had been dug. I got back in my car and drove further down the dirt road. I got out one more time to remove the crime scene tape that had been blocking the trail, then parked near the spot where the trailer had been found.

"Sorry about this," I said to Cara. "I'm just going to walk around and see if I can find the guy who owns that car, or at least see if he's been here."

"Don't worry about it. We'll get out and walk with you. If that's okay?"

"That'd be great."

There was still a chill in the air, and here and there in the shadows were patches of frost.

Cara scanned the area as Alvin trotted along at the end of his leash, sniffing the air as he went. "What are we looking for?"

"No idea," I said. "Something out of place."

"We're looking for a body, aren't we?"

"I have to admit that the idea crossed my mind. If we do find a body, don't let Alvin pee on it." Alvin ignored my comment and pulled right and left, trying to follow all the exotic smells.

We heard something crash through the undergrowth and we all jumped, but then I caught sight of the white tail bounding off through the woods.

"Deer," I said.

"Is that a house?" Cara asked, pointing at the old chimney sticking up through the vines.

"Yeah, what's left of it. There are some other outbuildings that have fallen into ruin too."

I saw trails going every which way, but they all looked like animal paths. I decided to walk around the old house. There was still enough of it remaining that someone could have hidden a body under the fallen timbers and rotten wood. Heart of pine was used to build most homes in the county before the Second World War and some of those posts and beams would still be there long after I was gone.

I thought I could hear a squeaking sound as I got closer to the ruins of the house. The ground was deep with vines and weeds so that I couldn't see where I was walking. I was glad that I'd put on hiking boots. Rattlesnakes and cottonmouths weren't a big concern this time of year, but the boots would help protect me from old nails and broken glass.

The noise seemed to get a little louder as I got closer to a hedge of azaleas that had gone feral. They had probably been planted when the house was in use, but now they were huge and woody and covered in purple blooms.

I had just brushed past some bushes when I felt my right foot touch… nothing. I went down hard. My left foot bent backward at an awkward and painful angle beneath me as my right foot tangled in the depths of the hole. My chest slammed into the ground, which kept me from falling all the way into the hole. A nail sliced into my right forearm.

The noise I'd been hearing turned into yelling from below. I felt something grab the boot on my right foot and I tried to kick it off, but I couldn't get any leverage. Whatever had clamped onto my foot wasn't going to let go. I was stuck. Without being able to free my right foot, I couldn't pull myself out of the hole.

I tried to establish contact with my captor, but he was screaming so loud and fast that I couldn't understand a word.

Cara came running around the corner of the house, dragging Alvin behind her. "Are you all right?" she asked.

"Not really. My foot fell in a hole and there's someone down there holding onto my leg." I could hardly hear myself over the screams of the man in the hole. "Shut up!" I yelled at him. "And let go of my foot!"

"No way!" he shouted back. "I've been stuck in this damn hole all night."

"I can't help you unless you let go of my foot. Damn it, I'm slipping. Do you want me to fall on top of you?"

"You ain't leaving me!"

"You aren't helping yourself, dumbass."

"What do you want me to do?" Cara asked, kneeling down beside me. I was using both hands to hold onto some wisteria vines, barely able to keep myself from slipping farther down into the hole.

"Get my phone off of my belt," I told her. As she reached around for my phone, Alvin decided to offer his support by coming up and licking my face. "Not helping," I told the Pug.

With a little awkward tugging, Cara finally managed to retrieve my phone. "Should I call 911?"

"Not yet. Try Darlene first."

"What are you doing?" shouted the man in the hole, who I assumed was Joel Patrick.

"Trying to get us out of this hole." I half thought about taking my gun and firing a round into the ground near the top of the hole to scare the moron into letting me go, and then I had a horrifying realization. My gun was in an ankle holster on the leg that he was currently clinging to. I hadn't wanted to carry my Glock 17 on my belt when I was planning on a long hike with Cara, so I'd strapped a smaller Glock 43 on my ankle. Now my nerves were humming. This cretin, and possible murderer, was just a few inches from my only handgun.

Cara found the speed dial for Darlene. I was rethinking the 911 call, but I knew that Darlene lived close by, and calling dispatch might get me the rookie of the day, which would be less than helpful.

"Let go of my leg or I'm going to have my friend up here start dropping stuff down on top of your head. Do you hear me?"

"You bastard!" he yelled.

I toyed with the idea of telling him I was a deputy, but I wasn't sure of his reaction. I figured it was better to not muddy the water while in my current awkward situation.

Cara gave Darlene a short synopsis of the situation, then hung up. "She's on her way. She said maybe ten minutes. Is there anything I can do?" she asked.

"Find a couple of bricks," I suggested and she headed off with Alvin toward the chimney.

"Did you hear me?" I shouted down at my ball and chain. "My friend is going to get a couple of bricks from the old chimney. If you don't let me go, I'll have her drop them down on top of you."

"Don't you dare," was the answer I got.

"Try me." To say my position was uncomfortable would be an understatement. My arm was bleeding and I was wondering how badly I'd injured my left foot *this* time. I sighed and looked up to see Alvin staring at me from about six inches in front of my nose.

"Got 'em," Cara said.

"Good. Tie Alvin up so he doesn't fall in the hole and then come over here and kneel down."

Cara was back in a second and edged her way carefully to the hole.

"Hold the brick over the hole," I told her. "Look up!" I shouted down to the man in the hole. "Do you see that brick? Now listen carefully. I'm a deputy with the Adams County Sheriff's Office."

"Just my damned luck," the man whined.

"I'm ordering you to release my foot. If you don't, I'm going to have to ask this woman to let the brick go. Do you understand?"

"Screw you!" he shouted.

I started to count to three, but on two I felt my foot released. "He let go. Give me a hand," I said to Cara. She put the bricks down and helped me drag myself out of the hole.

Once I was standing I assessed my injuries. Besides the three-inch-long cut on my arm, I'd definitely twisted my left ankle. It hurt, but I could walk on it. I eased carefully back to the side of the hole.

"We'll be back in a few minutes to get you out. Are you Joel Patrick?"

A long string of curse words came from the darkness.

"Right. We'll be back. Don't go anywhere," I told him and another stream of obscenities followed.

I limped back to the car and pulled the first aid kit from my trunk while Cara untied Alvin. By the time I'd cleaned and bandaged the cut on my arm, Darlene pulled up beside us. I filled her in on our suspect and the situation.

"I've got some rope in the back," Darlene said and, sure enough, she pulled a coil of climbing grade rope and two pairs of gloves out of her trunk. "Never know when you might need to rappel down a building," she said with a smile.

We walked back to the hole. I started clearing around it to get some sense of where the true edges were.

Hearing our approach, the man in the hole became a lot more friendly. "Hey! Hey, buddy, I was just kidding. I've been down here awhile. I'll tell you anything you want to know. Just get me out. Yeah, yeah, I'm Joel. Guess you found my car…"

The words continued to flow as we prepped the rope. I have to admit that I thought about questioning him while he was still down there, but thought better of the idea. A defense attorney would probably frame that as coercive.

"We're going to drop a rope down to you. Tie it under your shoulders," I said, tossing the rope down the hole. Darlene would be the anchor, and I'd pull him up. "Let us know when you have it tied off." I could have given him some hints on how to tie the rope comfortably, but I must have forgotten.

"Okay, I'm ready," he shouted.

"Ready when you are," I said to Darlene. She nodded. "Hang on!" I shouted and we began to pull.

A few minutes later Joel Patrick was sprawled out on the weeds a couple of feet from the hole. The lower half of his body was muddy and he was missing a shoe. The rest of him wasn't much cleaner and he stank.

"Oh, thank God," he moaned and hugged the earth. He was middle-aged and balding.

He started to get up, but I motioned him back down. "You can just lay there for a minute," I said. Reluctantly, I patted him down, wishing there was running water nearby to wash my hands off afterward. I found a knife, a wallet, keys and some change.

"Where's your phone?"

"Where do you think? Under about two feet of mud at the bottom of that damn well. Hey, what gives? You rescue a guy and treat him like a convict?" he whined. Apparently he had only three vocal inflections: yelling, begging and whining.

"I've got ten bucks that says you'll be a convict before this is all over," I said.

"No way, man. I'll take that bet. I ain't done nothing wrong."

"Trespassing at the very least. Assaulting a law enforcement officer. I'm sure we can think of some others," Darlene said. "You're lucky that smelling like crap isn't against the law."

Cara and Alvin were sitting a ways off, watching the show. Cara actually looked like she was enjoying it. Alvin simply looked bored.

"Want me to cuff him?" Darlene asked.

"Come on…" More whining.

"No. We'll see how cooperative he is." Which wasn't true. I had already decided that, if nothing else, he was going to be held overnight as a material witness.

"What's your name?"

"You know what my name is. Why do cops always ask questions they already know the answer to?" He shook his head. "Can I get a coat or something? And I really gotta get cleaned up. I was stuck in the mud at the bottom of that hole all night."

Darlene moved into his personal space. They were about the same size, so she could get nose to nose with him. *She must be holding her breath*, I thought.

"Don't be stupid. 'Cause I can tell you've been through

the process. I don't have to run your record to see that. It's written all over you. So you know how this works. Only a stupid person would piss us off by not answering our questions. You aren't going to smell a bit better after you spend a night in jail." Darlene backed up, no doubt to take a breath.

He held up his hands in surrender. "Yeah, you're right. I guess I'm just a little rougher for wear after the night I've had." He turned to me. "I'm sorry for the foot thing. I was just scared you were going to leave me down there." His new charm campaign was as transparent as a window without glass.

"What's your name?" I started over, ignoring his disingenuous apology.

"Joel Howard Patrick. I'm forty-one years old and was born in Panama City." He paused for a second and then added, "I've had various misunderstandings with the law over the course of my life. I'm sure you all have them written down somewhere, so I won't bother trying to recite them."

I opened his wallet and took out his driver's license. Handing it to Darlene, I said, "Check and see if he has any outstanding warrants."

"I shouldn't have! If I do, they're mistakes. I've been keeping my nose clean," he protested and started following Darlene, who'd moved off to make the call over her radio.

"Not so fast," I said, pulling him back. "We'll continue our conversation over here."

He looked uncomfortably from me to Darlene and back again.

"What are you doing out here?"

"I'm looking for property to buy," Joel said smoothly. I didn't believe it for a second, but I was planning on having a more thorough conversation at a later date, so I didn't press him on it. Sometimes hearing the lies people told could be as informative as the truth.

"Where were you on the night of Monday, March seventh and the morning of March eighth?"

"With friends," Joel said, a little too quickly. "Hey, police dogs are getting smaller," he added, nodding over at Alvin.

"That is one lame attempt to distract me. Let's agree to respect each other's professional skills. You treat me like a competent law enforcement officer and I'll treat you like the career criminal you are."

"Oh, a dagger to my heart. Sure, whatever. But I have friends that will back me up. In fact, you know one of my friends. Her name is Marcy," he said, confirming my suspicions. Apparently he was willing to throw her under the bus.

"You also have another old friend here in town. Jane Parrish. Unfortunately, her father was killed not two hundred yards from where I pulled you out of that hole," I said and had the satisfaction of seeing him frown.

"Yeah, who would have thought they wouldn't fill in an old well like that? I should sue the county and the Parrish family."

"Try it. Juries around here don't like trespassers." Damn it. He'd managed to get me off track. "Again, I need to know when, where and who for Monday night and Tuesday morning."

"You're boring me to death. Look, I didn't murder Parrish. I'll save you some time on that. I didn't kill either Parrish. The old man or the son."

"But you do know Jane?"

"I knew her a long time ago. Her family was a bunch of jerks. Back then I just wanted a good time."

"And what do you want now?"

"I'm just trying to get along and not hurt anybody."

Darlene came back. "He's not wanted for anything today. But he has a string of arrests and a few convictions that stretch back to the days when he had a full head of hair," Darlene said.

"Ouch," Joel said, smoothing down his comb over. "Now can I go?"

Darlene ignored him. "Most of the convictions are for

fraud. Two arrests were for fighting, but those were the only ones for violent crimes and the charges were dropped."

"Where are you staying?" I asked him.

"An amazing four-star establishment called the Roads Best. Room 214 which, for all of its shortcomings, does have a shower that delivers very hot water. I'd like to go make use of it." He paused and then added, "Please." This last word actually sounded sincere.

I held up his driver's license. "Okay, you can go, but I'm going to hold on to this. I'll give it back to you tomorrow morning at nine o'clock at the sheriff's office."

"You can't do that."

"Or I can give it back to you now and you can spend the night at the jail being held as a material witness in two murders," I bargained.

"You're serious."

I stared at him, holding out the driver's license. He looked at the card, then shrugged.

"Whatever. I'll see you in the morning then," he grumbled.

I gave him back his keys and wallet. After he'd walked off, Darlene turned to me. "You didn't ask him about the break-in at Albert Griffin's or the shooting at your place."

"No. I don't want him to know how much we already know about his activities. We'll toss all that at him tomorrow morning. I plan on grilling him until he's well done to burnt," I said between gritted teeth. I was still holding a grudge over him clamping onto my foot.

"The jail will appreciate you letting him get clean in the hotel's shower."

Cara and Alvin had walked over to join us. "You ready to get our day back on track?" I asked her.

"I don't know. This was pretty entertaining," she said with a grin.

"Aren't you a cutie?" Darlene said, bending down to scratch Alvin behind the ears.

"Appreciate your help," I told Darlene.

"Anytime. What are Sunday mornings for if not pulling a suspect out of a well? I'll run by the Roads Best and make sure that's where he went."

"See you in the morning."

Ten minutes later Cara and I were back on the road.

"You still haven't told me where we're headed," she prodded.

"Torreya State Park. It's only about half an hour from here. Trust me, you'll love it."

"What an amazing view," Cara said, once we were standing on the high bluff overlooking the Apalachicola River. "You'd expect to see something like this in north Georgia, not Florida."

Her red hair was blowing in a gentle breeze and her blue eyes were wide with awe. I smiled, loving the sight of her. I put my arms around her as we turned to look at the charming Gregory House that rose behind us. The white two-story house had been built in 1849 on the other side of the river, but the Civilian Conservation Corps had moved it to the bluff in the 1930s when the state park was developed.

"Do you want to walk the trails?" I asked. The sky was clear blue and the air held the pleasant warmth of early spring

"I'm game. But what about you? How's your ankle?"

"It's sore, but not too bad. I think I can make it. Alvin, you in?" I asked the Pug, who was too busy sniffing the ground to look up and enjoy the view.

The first part of the trail was steep as it dipped down to within fifty feet of the river elevation.

"I can't believe I haven't come over here before this," Cara marveled.

"During the nineteenth century, this was considered one of the possible locations of Eden," I told her.

"Really?"

"Yep. There are hundreds of rare species along this part

of the river. All of this area has these steep ravines where creeks have eroded the ground. They allow plants and animals to be cooler in the summer and warmer in the winter."

"I didn't know you had a botanist side," she kidded me as we navigated the rough earthen trail.

"I came camping here with the Boy Scouts a few times. I admit, it always made me feel like I lived in a special place."

"Eden. I can understand why they might have thought that on a… visceral level. The woods and the river are beautiful, wild and comforting all at the same time," Cara said.

The trail widened a little and I took her hand. "I like seeing the world through your eyes." I told her. She laughed lightly. "What's funny?"

"I got to see the world through your eyes this morning. And I hate to admit it, but I found it kind of exciting."

"Oh, sure, it wasn't you that got stuck in the hole," I chided her good-naturedly.

"Are you ready to turn back? You're limping again," she said with concern.

I stopped and pulled her to me. "I'm not sappy enough to say that when I'm with you I don't feel any pain. But I can definitely say that being with you makes it all worth it." I gave her a long kiss, then pulled away and looked down. "Your heavy breathing is *not* making this more romantic," I told Alvin, who looked up at me with his tongue lolling out of the side of his mouth.

Walking back up the hill in the late afternoon sunlight, we stopped to read the historical markers placed where Confederate gun pits could still be seen. "War comes to Eden," Cara said thoughtfully.

I ended up carrying Alvin the final hundred yards of the trail back up the bluff. "I'm the one with the bum leg. You should be carrying me," I told him. He was unimpressed with my reasoning.

By the time we left the park, I was feeling like a new man.

Even a mini-vacation is still a vacation.

CHAPTER THIRTEEN

We were halfway back to my house when the text alert on my phone went off. Under my *I-have-nothing-to-hide* policy, I let Cara read it.

"It says: 'She's headed to your place. Sorry.'"

"Is it from Eddie?" I asked, knowing it was and, unfortunately, knowing who he was talking about.

"Is it Marcy?"

"Who else?" I answered, letting my foot fall a little heavier on the gas pedal. So much for the mini-vacation.

"You still haven't given her the book?" Cara asked.

"No, I haven't seen her. And it's not like I can put out a BOLO on her."

"Why not… oh."

"Exactly. It's really frowned upon for law enforcement officers to use our resources to track current or former significant others. They spent the better part of two hours in one of my academy classes explaining the deep shit you can get into if you let your personal life mix with your professional life."

"But you're starting to think she may have a connection to the murders, aren't you?"

"And that's a problem. If I tell anyone that, the next

thing I'll be told is that I should step back and let someone else handle the case." It was very frustrating. The ethics surrounding the separation of work and personal life were a lot more complex in a small community like Adams County where everyone knew everyone or, at most, there was just one degree of separation.

"I can be impartial where Marcy is concerned. Unfortunately, she can't be."

"I don't want to criticize, but it *does* look like your blood pressure goes up every time you mention her name," Cara said matter-of-factly.

"I admit that there is still some… pain, mixed with a little fear, from my past relationship with her. But I'm still able to make rational decisions where she's concerned. What the hell?!"

This exploded out of my mouth when we rounded the corner before my place and I saw Marcy kicking the lock on my gate. Her car was parked in the driveway, preventing me from pulling in. I had to pull off on the side of the road.

"Stop that!" I yelled when I got out of the car.

Marcy looked up, her face red and her breathing labored from kicking my gate. As soon as she saw me, she started toward me, stomping her feet and clearly taking the offensive.

Realizing what I was walking into, I held up my hand. "Don't come any closer," I told her in my best authoritarian voice.

"What? You going to be the big cop and arrest me? You're the one who stole my book. Give it back. Now!"

She kept coming. My choices were narrowing with the seconds. I could retreat or defend. So I chose option three: capitulate.

"You're right. I'll give you your book. I didn't know that I had it the last time we talked." I was holding up both hands, palms out, in the traditional posture of surrender. I could only hope that she was in the mood to take prisoners.

"You have it?" she asked suspiciously. "Here?"

"Yes. If you'll let me get by you, I'll unlock the gate and we can go up and get the book. *Treasure Island*, right?" I was speaking in the same voice I reserved for drunks and the mentally challenged.

"Okay. But no tricks." She backed up and then seemed to notice Cara sitting in my car. "Who's that?" she asked, suspicious all over again.

"A friend. Let's just go up to the house and get this over with." I wanted to question her about her choice of friends and what they'd been up to together, but this didn't seem like the right time.

"Yeah, don't think I'm jealous," Marcy said.

What? I thought. *How delusional are you?* But she turned around. I followed her and opened the gate under her watchful glare.

Once I was back in my car, I turned to Cara. "I told her I'd give her the book. She's obviously madder than a mad hatter."

"She's a little scary," Cara agreed.

"You can stay in the car," I said, pulling in and following Marcy up the driveway.

"No. I want to watch the show. You might need backup."

I parked well clear of Marcy's car so that she would have no trouble backing up and turning around, no matter what kind of mood she was in when she left.

She was standing on the small porch, looking around nervously. Cara and I got out of the car, Alvin in tow, and cautiously joined her on the porch. I moved past Marcy with my key out.

"I'm Cara," I heard behind me. I hoped a fight wouldn't break out before we made it inside.

"Right. Guess you know I'm Marcy. I had him long before you."

I cringed and swung the door open quickly.

"Come on in. I'll get the book and you can be on your way."

"Trying to get rid of me?" Marcy asked.

"Frankly, yes," I said soberly as I left the room.

I came back to find Cara and Marcy trying hard not to look at each other. I held out the book and Marcy came to grab it out of my hand.

I pulled it back. "Not so fast. I want a couple of answers first."

"You bastard!" Marcy shouted and tried to grab the book. I held it up out of reach.

"Stop! Or I swear I'll burn it." I was speaking the truth and Marcy knew it. She stopped and really looked at me for the first time that afternoon. I swear she actually growled at me.

"I want you to answer a few questions, that's all. You have some very dodgy friends. I met one of them this morning."

I could see by the look in her eyes that I now had her full attention. "Who?" Before I could answer, she launched into damage control mode. "I grew up here. I've got a lot of friends. You're just picking on me 'cause you're still pissed about us breaking up. I ought to report you. Oh, yeah, your daddy's the sheriff, so that won't work. Well, screw you!"

I let her rant herself out, then asked, "How do you know Joel Patrick?"

"Who says I know him?"

"He does."

"He's lying," she pouted.

I sighed. "Let's sit down." I'd decided to try a different tack.

"Why?"

"Because we used to be friends, and I want to make sure that you aren't getting into something that you're going to regret," I said reasonably.

"You don't control my life! Just 'cause we were friends once..." She continued to rant, then roughly swept a pile of books and papers off of my dining room table and onto the floor.

"She's not crazy," Cara said, loudly enough to be heard over Marcy's ravings. I think that both Marcy and I had forgotten that Cara was in the room. She'd been standing back out of the way, but now she stepped forward. I winced, thinking: *This can't be good.*

"Why the hell is she even here?!" Marcy shouted and waved her arms.

"This is just an act. How long have you been using the crazy girlfriend routine to get your way?" Cara asked calmly.

I stepped between them. "I don't think—" I started, but Cara gave me a look that stopped me.

"Let the woman talk. I've seen crazy and she's not crazy," Cara argued. I wasn't so sure she was right.

It put Marcy in the awkward position of either agreeing with Cara or arguing that she really was crazy. I could see that Marcy was weighing the pros and cons and, in the moment, I realized that Cara might have a point. If Marcy had really been insane, she probably would have just attacked Cara when confronted rather than make a reasoned decision.

"I don't know what business this is of yours," Marcy came back with, but she sounded less sure of herself than before.

"Simple. I'm his girlfriend. You're… apparently an old friend of his. He's trying to help you, so I'm trying to help him help you."

"I don't need you people's help. I just need that damn book!" Marcy was back at full volume.

"And you aren't getting the book until you answer a few of my questions," I put in.

"Screw it!" Marcy flung up her hands and then threw herself down into one of the dining room chairs.

I carefully sat down in the chair next to her while Cara sat across the table from us.

"I don't want her here," Marcy blurted out.

Cara didn't move. "Why? So you can try to manipulate Larry without someone who sees through you watching? The difference between you and me is that I don't think Larry's an idiot, and you do."

Marcy clearly wasn't as good with women as she was with men. I don't think she'd spent much time around the female of the species. She glared at Cara, but kept her mouth shut for a change.

"How do you know Joel?" I forged ahead. Slowly Marcy took her eyes off of Cara and looked at me.

"I met him down in South Beach."

"You were working there?" I asked very gently.

"Yeah, I was bartending. Made a lot of money in tips too," she said defiantly.

"When did you meet him?"

"I don't know. Last fall. He likes to be the big man on the beach," she said, then added, "but he throws money around when he's got it. So that's cool." Marcy slumped down in the chair, which I took as a good sign. She was relaxing.

"Did you come up here with him?"

"Nah, he followed me," she said.

"Why did he follow you?" I asked.

"Not what you think." Marcy sat back up. "He wasn't fu… having sex with me or anything. He doesn't have that much money."

I had to keep from smiling at that last comment. What was really funny was that Marcy didn't understand how it made her look. Some people…

"So why do you think he came up here?"

She sighed and looked uncomfortable. "Just because."

"Is it because of the gold?"

The minute I mentioned the gold she sat bolt upright in her chair and her eyes went wide while her mouth dropped open. "I knew it!" she said. "Give me that book."

She reached over, trying to grab the copy of *Treasure Island.* I'd placed the book toward the other end of the table. I put my hand on it.

"I'm not after the gold. I don't even believe it exists," I told her, putting her in a quandary. She wanted to argue with me, but she really didn't want me to believe that it existed.

"Well, that's your opinion. I don't even know how you know about the treasure." More pouting.

"Marcy, the story of Nazi gold has been in the local paper for decades. Everybody knows about it," I reasoned.

"Yeah, but not that I'm looking for it." She looked away as though even she was a little embarrassed that she believed in the legend.

"What made you decide to leave your job down south and come up here looking for the gold?" I asked, genuinely perplexed.

"I'm not telling you nothin' about the gold." Her teeth clenched and her eyes narrowed to slits. "I came up here because my daddy is dying." Something about the way she said that had a ring of truth to it.

"When did Joel come up here?"

"Don't know." She still had her teeth clenched, afraid I was trying to trick her into revealing the secrets of the Nazi gold.

"I'm investigating two murders. I don't care about gold. I'm going to level with you. Joel is a serious suspect in my investigations. When did you first learn that he was up here?"

"Guess about two weeks ago," Marcy said, which put him up here in plenty of time to be the murderer or an accomplice.

"You sort of let on that he came here for the gold. How did he hear about it?"

She stared at me, no doubt trying to decide if she would give anything away by telling me the truth. "I might have said something to him," she finally admitted, frowning.

"You mentioned the fact that you had a lead on the gold and that's why he came to Adams County?"

"I didn't say nothin' about a lead."

"Right now to me or to him?" I asked and the question seemed to confuse her.

"Not to you," Marcy said, and I took that as a yes to the

fact that she told Joel about a lead.

"Who else is involved in this gold hunt?"

"I'm not saying nothing else," she said, folding her arms across her chest like a petulant child. I could have mentioned Eddie, but I didn't want to spoil my CI's cover.

"A man shot at me down by my gate on Wednesday night. What do you know about that?"

I watched her carefully, and she seemed really surprised and interested in the information. She leaned forward and put her arms on the table. "Someone shot at you? You sure it has to do with the gol… me?"

"I'm sure that the shooting has to do with the murders, and I'm pretty sure that the murders have to do with the hunt for gold," I told her and watched her consider this information.

"I don't know anything about a shooting," she said simply.

"Did you tell him about the book?"

"I… Maybe… You know I kinda talk too much when I've been drinking."

"Is there anyone else involved? Anyone you know of?"

"Can't say. You said yourself that the story's been around forever." She paused, then added, "Joel's got a big mouth when he's been drinking too, and that's like every night." Marcy tried to keep her eyes from darting around, but she couldn't. She knew a lot more than she was saying.

"What was your relationship to George Pike?" I asked.

"Who?" was Marcy's totally unconvincing answer.

"Don't be stupid. We can easily look it up."

"Okay, he was my grandfather. He stole that gold. I know he did," she said with pride.

I didn't know what having that information did for me, but it helped explain some of her interest in the gold. Not that she needed any incentive to be interested in gold. She still hadn't mentioned Eddie, who I knew wasn't the shooter, but certainly seemed to be involved in this crazy gold hunt. Having a sit-down with Eddie was moving to the top of my to-do list.

I pulled up a picture on my phone of the white pickup that had been stolen, used to haul the backhoe, driven by my shooter and burned up at the county sandpit. The owner had sent us the photo. I showed it to Marcy. "Have you seen this truck?"

As soon as she saw the picture her eyes started moving all around the room again, avoiding mine.

"Marcy, this is really important. The person who was driving this truck is the same man who shot at me and is deeply involved in these murders. You need to help me. You need to separate yourself from him."

"What are you saying?" She tried to sound tough, but I could hear a little hesitation in her voice.

"I'm saying that by coming clean right now, you can keep yourself from going down with this guy. I know that you've had your troubles, but nothing like what's been happening this week. I'm throwing you a lifeline."

The gears were turning slowly. She looked left, then right and back again. I was very surprised when she looked directly at Cara. They locked eyes for a moment before Marcy looked down at the table. I wondered what type of secret message had passed between them. I made a mental note to ask Cara about that.

"I don't know anything about the truck," Marcy said in a tone that I recognized from years earlier. She'd made up her mind not to talk about the truck and the person behind it, and I doubted that I could change that.

"Where were you on the night of March seventh and the morning of the eighth?"

"I don't remember," she answered sullenly.

"Come on, you aren't even trying to answer my questions," I said and, absentmindedly, moved the book a little farther away from her. Her eyes followed the book.

"I mean it. I don't remember anything after about seven o'clock on the seventh." I heard something in her voice that was new. She sounded confused.

"What happened?" I gave her a more open-ended question.

"I thought I'd been raped," Marcy said, looking down at the floor.

"What?" I said, astonished at this admission.

"But I wasn't. I just thought… Maybe." She wasn't making a lot of sense.

"What made you think you'd been raped?"

"I had a drink and just kinda crashed. I didn't wake up till the next day, and I… I know what it feels like to be drugged. Someone had put something in my drink. So… I thought…"

"But they hadn't? Who did it?"

"I don't know, and if I find out they're going to pay," she said through gritted teeth. I didn't think it was an accident that she'd been drugged on the night that someone had attempted to dig up the gold.

"Could it have been Joel?"

"I… He wasn't there when it happened." She looked defeated. I almost felt sorry for her.

"Marcy, you know more than you're telling me. Maybe not about that night, but about other aspects of this case."

"Says you!" The fiery Marcy flared up like a struck match.

"Marcy, this man may be dangerous. There are two ways that this could bite you in the ass. One is that you will be pulled in as some sort of accomplice and wind up in jail. The other possibility is that you'll wind up like Hank and Joe Parrish." I let that sink in. I thought for a moment that she might change her mind, but then her eyes narrowed and grew cold.

"I told you, I don't know anything else. Give me my damned book!"

We talked for a few more minutes, mostly just me issuing warnings about Joel and trespassing before I reluctantly handed the book over to Marcy. As soon as she had the book in hand, she wanted to leave. Oddly, I had mixed feelings about seeing her run off. On the one hand, she was a loose cannon in my life that I really didn't need. But on the other, she was someone I'd known most of my life, in a vulnerable moment, and I felt a bit sorry for her.

I turned to Cara after watching Marcy drive away. "Well?"

"She really believes that she can find the gold, and no matter what her brain is saying about the dangers, she's going to go forward at full speed," Cara summed up.

"That's what I'm afraid of."

I pulled out my phone and called dispatch. After some quick chitchat with the dispatcher, I told her that I wanted patrol to make regular swings by the property near the railroad tracks and to keep an eye out for anyone trespassing.

"What was that look that passed between you two?" I asked Cara after I hung up.

"I think she was just looking for some support."

"It's been an interesting day."

"I could probably get out to the range with Pete sometime soon," Cara said suddenly.

I'd been wanting her to take firearms training with Pete for a few weeks now. "I'll let him know," I said, hiding a smile.

CHAPTER FOURTEEN

Darlene arrived a few minutes after I got to my desk on Monday morning.

"You're in early," she observed.

"Want to have our ducks in a row when we talk to Joel, or be ready to hunt him down if he doesn't show," I said, clicking the print icon on my screen so that we'd have a large picture of the stolen truck to show him. As the page printed, I filled Darlene in on my meeting with Marcy. She nodded and shook her head at all the right places.

"The gold. That's just crazy…"

While we waited, I emailed a picture of Joel Patrick to Albert Griffin and asked him if he could be the man that broke into his home. He answered back immediately with an apology that he just couldn't be sure.

Joel was half an hour late. Darlene and I were just getting ready to ride out to the Roads Best and see if we could find him when we got a message from the desk sergeant that Joel was waiting.

We brought him back to an interrogation room. Sometimes I like to do preliminary questioning in the more informal atmosphere of one of the conference rooms, but with Joel we decided that it would be best to skip the frying pan and throw him straight into the fire.

"Hey, I'm right here, just like I told you," he bragged as we took him back. "Wow, am I under arrest or something?" he asked when I opened the door to the small, windowless interrogation room.

"Don't try to kid a kidder," Darlene told him. "We've seen your record. You know when you're being arrested and when you aren't."

He sat down with both of us across from him.

"This conversation is being recorded, and I'd like you to say that you are here of your own free will." I stopped and looked at him. He shrugged. "You need to say it out loud."

"Mostly, I'm here of my own free will," he allowed.

"Are you willing to voluntarily answer questions?" Darlene pushed.

"Yes, yes, yes, I love talking to you all. I really want to be here with such a lovely lady and a great guy like Deputy Macklin." He paused. "How's that?"

"Fine," I said, and we had him go through the rest of the introduction stating his name and vital statistics.

"Marcy told you I was with her when the murders occurred," he stated.

"Funny, but no, she didn't," I responded. He looked aggravated at this news, but not surprised.

"Following up on that, I'd like you to give me the names of anyone else who can back up your story."

"There was Marcy… Let me think… A couple of other people, but I can't recall their names."

"I suggest you think hard and try and come up with them," I said, already tired of his conman persona.

"No. Nothing," he said.

"I think you should know that we are investigating two homicides," I told him and took out the autopsy photos of both victims. I laid them out on the table so that Joel would have to look up or turn his head to avoid looking at them. He winced and began talking to the space above my head.

"I don't know anything about these people or how they

died."

"Would you be willing to take a polygraph test to prove that?" I shot back.

He frowned and looked directly into my eyes. "You and I both know that those tests are not proof of anything. So, no. I won't take one."

I wasn't at all surprised and, honestly, a man as comfortable at lying as he was could probably have passed one anyway.

"Have you ever fired a crossbow?" Darlene asked.

She and I had agreed that our main strategy for the interview would be to throw questions at him from all directions constantly, trying to keep him off balance by asking the unexpected. From the look on his face, so far so good.

"Ehhh, maybe once when I was a kid." He glanced around nervously and I wasn't sure if it was caused by the pictures on the table or the question itself.

"Let's go over your history with Jane Parrish and her family. When did you meet her?" I asked.

"Jane? Wow. That's ancient history. I guess that was at Panama City Beach. I must have been in my early twenties and Jane was a little younger. She turned heads in a bikini, I can tell you that. She had me from the moment I saw her."

"What was the nature of your relationship?" Darlene asked dryly.

"She called and I came." He actually blushed. "No pun intended. I swear. What can I say? I was smitten. In fact, I followed her all the way back here."

"Where you met her family?" Darlene asked for clarification.

"That didn't go so well. I didn't realize that they were big fish in a small pond. Every one of them told me to go away at one point or another. Kind of stupid for me to hang out, really. Jane just put up with me in Panama City, but when she saw her family's reaction to me, she decided that she wanted to be with me. Works that way sometimes," he said, sounding very pleased with himself.

"You argued with her family?" Darlene was being cold as ice to this has-been Lothario.

"You could say that. First off, her father tried to work me to death on his farm. But in those days, I was seriously buff. It's ruined my skin, but all those days on the beach kept me fit enough to keep up with these country boys. I even got where I kind of liked the work. I read a lot back then too. Kind of got the whole back-to-earth thing going."

"You got in a fight with Hank Senior?" I prodded.

"Yes. Likely coming to the farm was a mistake. Jane wanted someone that would take her away from her yokel family. When I got into the work, she started pushing me away again. Look, I was young and didn't think my stink stunk, if you know what I mean, so after putting in all the hard work, I was a little pissed that I was getting the heave-ho. Her father caught me hanging around the house once too often and decided to teach me a lesson. Believe me, he started the fight."

"He started it and, from what we heard, he finished it," I pushed.

"Not really. I decided that if it looked like he was the big bad man beating up on her poor boyfriend, Jane might go back to wanting me. Maybe we could go somewhere away from this redneck retreat," Joel finished, but I wasn't so sure I believed him.

"How did that work out for you?" Darlene asked, her voice dripping with sarcasm.

"Not well. But that's how she'd twisted my brain all up."

"Sounds like she'd twisted some other part of your anatomy."

"Very funny."

"The point of the story, though, is that you got kicked to the curb by father and daughter?" I asked.

Joel looked at me, unwilling to allow that he'd been beat. But after a ten count he looked down at the floor. "Pretty much."

"So you were pissed."

He laughed. "Sure I was, twenty years ago. If you'd dug the old man's body up from a grave twenty years old, you might have a point. Jeez, if I held grudges for that long, I wouldn't have time for doing anything else except updating my blacklist."

"I guess you've made some enemies over the years. Conmen seldom make friends," Darlene stated. She'd spent quite a while that morning going over Joel's arrest and conviction records.

"I like to think of myself as a businessman."

"And I like to think of myself as Miss America," Darlene muttered, almost causing me to laugh out loud.

"On to the second murder," I said, to cover up my laughter. "Where were you Friday morning?"

"Ha!" Joel exclaimed, looking like he'd just bowled a strike. "I was in an argument with one of your lot."

"How's that?" I asked, already sure that he must have a pretty good alibi by the way he was acting.

"That bastard at the motel was trying to get me evicted. Some deputy pounded on my door at seven-thirty in the morning. The damn manager wanted me gone before the weekend, like that dump was going to have a rush on it. Luckily, I'd gotten some cash and was able to settle up. But just check your records," he said triumphantly. I made a note to do just that, but I figured he had this one locked up. Though it wouldn't necessarily rule out the break-in at Mr. Griffin's.

It was time to shake the conversation up again. "When did you first hear about the gold?" I asked.

Joel's mouth fell open. I think he'd planned on saying something, but couldn't think of what. "What gold?" was the not-very-clever answer he finally came up with.

"The gold that you were looking for on the Parrish property down by the railroad tracks. The gold that you were looking for when you fell into an abandoned well," I shot back.

"Damn it, Marcy," he said and looked down at the table. His eyes landed on the pictures of the corpses of the two Parrishes, causing him to look away. For the first time since I'd met him, he had lost his composure. Even after spending the night at the bottom of a well, he'd seemed more together than he was now.

"Yep, damn Marcy. Did she get you into this snipe hunt?" I asked.

"I'll talk about the murders. Murders which I have nothing whatsoever to do with, but if you continue to ask about gold, I'm going to walk out of here." Joel had lost his humorous demeanor. I was sure that he was an expert on jailhouse law, so pushing the point would only leave me with an empty interrogation room.

"Forgetting the gold for the moment, what is your relationship to Marcy Pike?"

"Just friends."

"Do you know of anyone that might have been involved in these murders?"

"No."

I put the picture of the truck next to the ones of the bodies. "Do you recognize this truck?"

Joel took a quick glance. His poker face was too good to tell me anything. "No," he said.

"You've never seen this truck?" Part of the point of this interview was to get him to give answers on the record that could be used later.

"I can't say that. This is the boondocks of the boondocks out here. Everybody drives a truck." He tapped the picture without looking down at it. "I could have passed this truck ten times and not remembered."

Of course, he had a valid point, but I was pretty sure he knew a lot more about this particular truck.

"Who else have you and Marcy been hanging out with while you've been in Adams County?"

"Mostly friends of Marcy's. But she's spent quite a bit of time with her family at the nursing home. You know her dad's dying?"

When he mentioned Marcy's dad, it made me think of her relationship to George Pike and that's when the proverbial light bulb went on.

"You're related to James Patrick!" I blurted out. Darlene had started to ask a question, but my mind had gone down the ancestor rabbit hole and I hadn't been listening.

Joel Patrick and Darlene both stared at me. It only took Darlene a second to catch up. "What is your relationship to James Patrick?" she fired at him.

"Who?" Joel asked weakly.

"James Patrick, the man who in 1946 was shot while trying to desert an Army train passing through Adams County."

"He was not trying to desert," Joel said before he could stop himself.

"But you don't want to talk about the gold," I asked, enjoying seeing him squirm.

"He didn't desert," Joel repeated.

"No, he didn't because another soldier shot him before he could." I rubbed a little salt in the wound. Apparently, it was too much because he stood up.

"If you aren't going to arrest me, I'm leaving."

"Have a good day, Mr. Patrick," I said, putting a little extra emphasis on his last name. "But don't leave town. We'll be watching you." With only a minor trespassing violation and no concrete evidence to connect him to the murders or the theft at Mr. Griffin's, we couldn't hold him, but I wanted him to know that we weren't finished with him.

After he left, Darlene smiled at me. "I should have gotten that connection," she said. "Nice. I think we got first blood."

"He sure is sensitive about James Patrick's good name. Grandfather?" I wondered.

"Easy enough to check," Darlene said. After five minutes on her computer she was able to confirm the relationship.

We spent the rest of the morning going over all the interviews and reports. Dr. Darzi had scheduled Joe's autopsy for one o'clock, so we headed for Tallahassee and grabbed tacos at Cabo's Island Grill before going to the hospital. I wasn't worried about eating before the mashed head autopsy. After the body I had found sautéing in a hot tub in January, I was pretty sure my stomach could handle just about anything else.

One of Dr. Darzi's interns ushered us into his inner sanctum where he was already prodding and poking at Joe Parrish's body.

"Are you purposefully trying to challenge me?" he asked as we joined him at the table. I couldn't keep my eyes from going to the spot where the head should have been. What remained had been laid out at the top of the corpse.

"We really try not to have unusual murders," I told him.

"I've had to look at the crime scene pictures in order to come to any conclusions. I should have come out there, but frankly I'm getting tired of driving to Adams County." Darzi paused. "Just kidding. I was giving a lecture in Atlanta, or I would have certainly been there.

"I did a thorough exam of the body. Unless he was poisoned, which we won't know until the toxicology report comes back, I think it is safe to say that a wound to the head caused his death." He held up a finger. "But that still leaves a pretty wide open door, as a professor of mine used to say. He could have been shot, he might have had a rod poked through his eye and into his brain, or maybe he was hit by an axe in the back of the head. There's the problem. Since someone took a concrete alligator and mashed the evidence of his mortal wound into putty, I can't tell from the body."

"So…" I prompted.

"So, I had to look at the crime scene photos to see what evidence there was. And what I could gather was that he was hit with an object while he was standing. Oh, and not that concrete alligator either. A smaller object, one that you can swing." Darzi made a motion like swinging a golf club over his head. "Probably from behind. You will have to consult with a blood splatter expert to get a better idea of the possible shape of the object used. They might be able to tell you if he was struck a second time before he fell to the ground. I think it's possible, but I'm not the man to say. The rest is obvious. Once on the ground someone, possibly the killer, mashed his head in. From the blood spray on the side of his truck, I would say that the first blow or two before he was on the ground would have been mortal. If not immediately, then certainly in a very short amount of time."

"My first thought when I saw the body was that someone was trying to conceal the identity of the victim," I thought out loud.

"But Joe's phone was in his pocket and his fingerprints matched the body," Darlene pointed out.

"There were two crowns that were not too badly damaged, and they matched the dental work that his dentist sent me. I'm pretty certain this is Joe Parrish. I think that someone hated him very much," Darzi said in a sad, wistful tone.

"Maybe they were trying to cover up evidence of the original weapon that was used," Darlene speculated.

"Curiouser and curiouser," I muttered. "Or maybe they were just trying to muddy the water."

"Without an identifiable wound, I can't give you an estimate of the killer's height, the direction of the blow or anything else. Again…"

"…with the blood splatter expert," I finished for him.

"Exactly. That's all the evidence we have for the fatal attack." He shrugged.

We hung around for a little more of the cut and dice, but the whole trip left me wondering why we'd bothered to come to the show. Darzi wasn't able to tell us anything we didn't already suspect.

Before we got back to the office, I received a text from Dad which said simply: *Come see me asap.* As frequently happened when I received commands from him like that, my juvenile first response was to ignore it. But my adult self was quick to remind me that he was also the sheriff and my boss, so I headed straight to his office.

Dad and Mauser were waiting for me. Dad did not look happy. Mauser, on the other hand, was the picture of contentment lying on the twin-sized bed Dad had made up for him. He was so comfortable that he didn't even get up to give me his usual excited greeting. He just lifted his eyelids and huffed in my general direction.

"Lazy dog," I muttered

"I got a call from Marge Parrish," Dad barked. "Her brother is missing."

I almost said, "No, he's not. I just saw what's left of him at the morgue," when I realized that he must be talking about Hank Junior. "Really?" was my lame answer.

"Do you realize that I'm in the middle of an election? Having the members of one of the most prominent farm families in the county being eliminated one by one is not helping." Dad held up a hand. "I know that sounds insensitive. But, damn it, after she called I had a moment when I wondered if this was someone trying to sabotage my reelection."

"That seems unlikely," I reasoned. "When did she call?"

"Right before I sent you the text."

"Did you send a deputy to take a report?"

"No. She's afraid that he's gone off the wagon and wants a discreet attempt to locate him first," Dad grumbled. He hated to play small-town politics. "Considering everything that has happened, I thought we could give the family a break and low-key the hunt."

"So you want me to go talk to her?"

"Exactly. And try not to turn this into another dead body. Where are you in the investigation?"

I described the steps we'd taken and got the occasional nod. When I got to the part about the gold, he just stared at me like I was crazy and the mention of Marcy's name caused him to throw his hands up in the air.

"People actually believe that nonsense? And Marcy Pike? That girl is nuts." Dad had never liked her, which had only caused me to be more attracted to her.

"Someone had it in for Joe. The level of damage was category five."

"Family?"

"Or a relationship that we haven't discovered yet," I said.

"Try and stay a safe distance from Marcy. Which brings up another related matter. Don't screw up the deal with Cara. Mauser and I like her."

Wow. I think that was the first time he'd ever approved of one of my relationships. Feeling highly uncomfortable with the direction of the conversation, I decided to turn the tables. "How's your relationship with Genie going?" I asked casually, referring to the manager of a restaurant in Tallahassee who I'd recently learned Dad might have a thing for.

If his eyes had been lasers, the look he gave me would have burnt a hole in my face. "At this point, that is none of your business. I'll let you know when my personal life concerns you." But he couldn't prevent a bit of a smile from creeping into those steely green eyes.

I still wasn't sure how I felt about Dad having a personal life. It was so unlike him. More than a little disturbed, I left his office and filled Darlene in on the situation with Hank Junior, then left to meet with Marge.

CHAPTER FIFTEEN

I found Marge pacing back and forth on the porch at the main house. When she saw me get out of the car, she hurried down the steps toward me.

"Hank's gone. Just gone!" Marge looked like she might break into tears at any moment. It was tough to watch this woman being emotionally torn apart by the events that were overtaking her family.

"Don't worry. We'll find him," I said, having no idea whether we would or wouldn't. Hundreds of people go missing every day—some of their own accord, some not.

"Before the murders, if this had happened I'd figure he was just off getting high. But now…"

"You could help by letting us make an official report and put out a bulletin. We could garner a lot more resources that way," I encouraged her.

"Maybe. But first just help me look." She looked like she was on the verge of collapse, but was still stubbornly insisting on doing this the hard way.

"Let's go in the house and talk for a minute." I guided her back up the stairs and into the dining room. "Where is Jane?"

"I don't know. I don't want to tell her yet. Hank has

always looked up to her. They were close as kids. Joe and I were the older children. The responsible ones. Hank cares so much what Jane thinks of him. If he hasn't fallen off the wagon, if there's a good reason for him being gone, I don't want to make things rougher for Hank. And if he's fallen off the wagon again, I want to give him a chance to come back without too much humiliation. I really can't blame him. We haven't even had the viewing for Dad, let alone a funeral, and now Joe. And you said that… he wasn't… presentable." Marge was rambling, but sometimes that's what people need. I let her vent her emotions a bit before sitting her down at the table.

"I need you to focus for me. I'll do what I can to find Hank, but you need to give me some information first. When was the last time you saw him?"

"Yesterday evening."

"What was he doing?"

"He was sitting in the kitchen. I thought that was odd. He wasn't eating. His appetite has been a bit better since he… got clean. But he's still not a big eater. I asked him if he wanted anything, and he just said no. I wasn't really in the mood to talk. All of us were… are still in shock."

"He wasn't doing anything?"

"Well, he did have his phone on the table. I wondered at the time if he was waiting for someone to call." *Or text*, I thought.

"What was his mood?"

"Like I said, I was still in a daze about Joe. I didn't pay much attention. I'm sorry."

"You asked him if he wanted something to eat. How did he answer? Was it curt? Polite?"

"Sort of matter-of-fact. Come to think of it, I did think he seemed a little emotionless. But who knows? What's normal with everything that's happened?" she asked, sounding baffled and confused.

"You didn't see him again?"

"No, but I did hear the back door open, and later I think

I saw a light on in his apartment."

"But you didn't see anyone else come or go, or hear him drive away?"

"I didn't want to stay here, but I thought I should and Clive said he'd stay with me. But my nerves were shot. The truth is, I took a couple of Valium and slept until eleven this morning. I feel so guilty, but I had to sleep."

"You did what you had to. Did your husband hear anything? Or notice anyone coming or going?"

"He didn't see Hank. I asked him that. But I didn't think to ask him about anyone else. I think he would have mentioned seeing someone else or if he'd heard Hank leave."

"Is Hank's truck here?"

"The truck he drives, yes. Daddy was very strict after all of Hank's troubles with drugs. Daddy gave him the keys to one of the farm trucks and told Hank that he'd throw him off the place if Hank so much as touched any of the other vehicles on the property. You might think Hank would have been offended, but he wasn't. He knew he'd screwed up too many times. Once, he ran an almost brand new tractor into a swamp. Cost Daddy a fortune to drag it out and get it running again."

These were stories that no one had mentioned earlier. Was Hank really okay with his father's strict rules? Or just tolerating them?

"Let's go look at his apartment. Do you have a key?" I asked, standing up.

"That was another thing that Daddy insisted on when Hank asked to move back in after drying out." Marge got up and I followed her into the kitchen. "He told Hank that he'd keep a key and inspect the apartment anytime he felt like it." She reached for a key hanging on a rack by the door.

"Your dad sounds like he was being a little harsh," I observed.

"Not really. Hank needed that strong hand. He'd gotten sober so many times before just to fall back into drugs and alcohol."

What you need and what you resent can often be the same thing, I thought. How badly was Hank chaffing under his father's thumb?

We went out the back door and up the stairs to Hank's apartment above the garage.

"Don't put the key in yet." I took out a pair of rubber gloves from my pocket and put them on. I should have considered what effect this would have on Marge. She actually whimpered as she watched me.

"I'm sorry. I'm just being overly cautious." I didn't know if I was or not. I reached out and tried the doorknob. Locked. I took the key from Marge and unlocked and opened the door. "Please don't touch anything," I instructed as we walked in.

I found the light switch and flipped it on. Having never seen the apartment before, I had no idea if the mess I was seeing was normal or not. There were books and papers all over the room, as well as pizza boxes and Coke bottles.

"Does this look normal to you?" I asked.

"Well… maybe a little messier than usual. He would ask Maria to come in occasionally. Daddy didn't have any problem with that."

We searched the room carefully and didn't find Hank's wallet, keys or phone. I told Marge that that was a good sign. It was evidence that Hank had left on his own. We also found a small stash of money.

"Thank you, God," she said, looking at the rolled up bills and counting out almost three hundred dollars. "If he had this money and didn't take it, that means he's not on drugs again," she said and then got an odd look on her face. "But if he's not on drugs, then where is he?"

"Who were his friends?" I asked.

"Ha! Druggies don't have friends. He burned all of his old friends long ago." Marge shook her head.

Marge had a point. Often a recovering addict's closest thing to a friend was someone else in recovery. "Did Hank go to AA meetings?"

"He did." The thought that there were more people to talk to caused her to rally a bit. "He sometimes went to the AA meetings in Calhoun. Actually, I think some of them were Narcotics Anonymous meetings."

"I know where they are." I looked at my watch. The groups usually met at several different times. Some of the new people would go to two meetings a day. Adams County wasn't as bad as some, but like the rest of rural America, we had a serious drug problem. Dad was adamant that the department support the rehab programs in the community. I even knew of one of our officers who attended meetings on a regular basis. I pulled out my phone and dialed Dill Kirby's number.

Dill was an old-timer. He'd been with the department for forty years and was now semi-retired, working the occasional special event or the front desk when we needed him. Years earlier he'd had to admit to having an alcohol problem. Now, once a year or more, Dad had him talk to the different shifts about how easy it could be for a deputy to go down the wrong path with drugs and alcohol. Dad hated it when he had to fire one of the deputies for substance abuse. He always looked on them as casualties of the job—a job that demanded you spend your life looking in the darkest corners of human nature.

"Hey, it's Larry. I'm trying to help out a woman whose brother's gone missing. He's had some issues with drugs and alcohol and has been going to local meetings. I was wondering if you could ask around and find out if anyone's seen him."

"What part of anonymous don't you understand?" Dill asked me good-naturedly.

"This is pretty urgent. It's Hank Junior."

I heard him take in a deep breath. "Damn. And his father and brother not even in the ground yet. You think something's happened to him?"

"Don't know. But he didn't have many friends. I thought his sponsor might have a clue. If you can just find out if they've heard from him. If he's safe, then everyone will be happy."

"I hear you. There's a meeting at the First Methodist in an hour. The way home meeting, we call it. It's very tempting to stop and get something you shouldn't on your way home from work. I'll find out. I've seen him at a couple of meetings recently. He seemed fine, but what's happened to his family in the last week would mess anyone up, let alone someone in recovery."

"Thanks."

I hung up and told Marge that a friend was going to follow up and give me a call if he found out anything. Just knowing something was being done seemed to give her some relief.

"What else can you do?" she asked me.

"I'm going to drive around a bit and see if I can find out anything. But if we haven't come up with any answers by nine o'clock, you're going to have to call Jane and anyone else that you can think of. We have to eliminate the possibility that they know something. After that, I would strongly urge you to let us pull out all the stops and start a major investigation into his disappearance."

I didn't tell her that I wasn't going to let that be optional. Hank Junior was a possible suspect in the deaths of his father and brother. One of the options that I had to consider was that he had fled in order to avoid being arrested.

"Okay. I can see that." Marge clenched her eyes shut and tapped her hand to her forehead. "No, no, I won't wait. I'll call Jane now. I can't worry about people's emotions and family politics." She dug her phone out of her pocket.

"Jane, have you seen Hank? Yes. Because I haven't seen him in a while, and he's not answering his phone." She listened to Jane for a few moments, then said, "No! No, you don't know that he's back on drugs. I certainly don't. Stop it!"

I could hear Jane's voice speaking loudly on the other end of the phone, even though I couldn't make out the words. They were coming fast and loud. Marge's eyes were moist and she wiped at them as she listened to the invective coming from the other end of the phone.

"I don't care what you think. He's our brother. Do what you want. Everyone in this family always has," Marge said and hung up. She clutched the phone tightly in her hand. "She hasn't seen or heard from him," she told me through tight lips.

Marge then assured me that she'd talked to any of their employees that might have seen Hank. She was also sure that they would have mentioned if they had seen a stranger or a car that they didn't recognize.

"That doesn't leave us with too many options," I said. "If he didn't take his truck, and no one picked him up, then he had to have walked."

Marge shook her head and stared out a window.

I thought about the property. From the house to the spot by the railroad tracks was a hike, but not that far. I decided that I wanted to go down there and look around. When I looked at Marge, I didn't feel like I could just leave her there. I had to remind myself that a sympathetic suspect can be as guilty as an unsympathetic one. Many investigations have gone down the rabbit hole by focusing on someone who didn't seem to be properly grieving or worried, while the real perpetrator was crying crocodile tears and egging on the police to try harder. Bad people can be very manipulative. At this point I had to keep an open mind about everyone, including Marge.

"I'm going to go check a couple things out. Why don't you come with me?" I suggested.

"Thank you."

The sun was low in the sky as I drove down to the woods by the railroad tracks.

"I should have thought about him coming down here," Marge said with a twinge of… what? Irritation? Frustration?

"He spent a lot of time down here when he was a kid. Always talking about that damn gold. Once he got that into his head, he just couldn't let it go. We all got sick and tired of hearing about it, but the more Daddy forbid him to hunt for it, the more determined Hank got."

I parked the car and we got out. It was a beautiful evening, cool and breezy. There wasn't any evidence of anyone else around, though the whole area had been walked over so many times in the last week that it would have been hard to tell. We walked back toward the ruins of the house.

"Watch out, there's an old well out here someplace," Marge said.

"Yeah, I know where that is," I said, then gave her a highly edited explanation of how I knew that, without any details about who we found in the well.

"We should have fenced this area off years ago. The old house was in pretty good shape when we were kids. When Hank was in high school, he and his friends used to hang out in it, drinking and smoking. Probably doing other things," Marge said as we poked around.

"You didn't ever believe in the legend of the gold?" I asked her.

"Ha! Only for a little longer than I believed in Santa Claus and the Easter Bunny. Ridiculous." She looked over toward the tracks. "You can just see the old railroad platform. Back in the day, the trains would stop and take on cotton and tobacco. A lot of the bigger farms had railroad loading docks back before everything started going by truck."

"When did you all start growing hay?"

"When shade tobacco became unprofitable. Granddad decided that he'd rather sell hay than start growing tomatoes or corn. Both are too much of a gamble. You're always trying to get in the first or the last crop to make the big money, and you have to invest in a lot of fertilizer, pesticides, irrigation. Hay's more predictable. You just have to be able to gauge the rain. Granddad was smart. He said that with weather prediction getting better all the time—this was back in the late sixties—it'd be safer then ever to grow hay."

"Your dad was good with that?"

"Daddy did whatever Granddad said. Period. It's what broke Mom down."

We'd walked back to where the backhoe had dug the holes.

"What a mess. We'll have to clean this up," Marge said. She seemed very comfortable with the idea of taking over the farm. I wondered if that was how it would work out. And I wondered how Jane and Hank would feel about that.

"You sound like you plan on running the farm," I said.

"Who else? Jane? Don't make me laugh. Hank? He has to work on his own problems. I don't think he has the time or the inclination to take on the business." She sounded very sure of herself. "Daddy was killed over there?"

We'd walked to the very edge of the woods. She was pointing about twenty degrees too far south.

"It was closer to over there," I said, indicating the spot where we found the body. Was this a ploy, pretending to not know exactly where her father's body had been found? Looking at the spot, I could clearly see where the hay had been trampled by all of the crime scene techs and deputies. It seemed like she should have seen that too. Or maybe I was just over-thinking it.

"I don't think Hank's here," Marge said softly.

An idea occurred to me. "Try calling him."

She looked at me for a moment as if she was going to ask why, but then she took out her phone and hit the speed dial button. "Voicemail," she said.

"Let's head back to the car."

When we got to the spot where the trailer and backhoe had been parked, I asked her to call again.

"Oh," she said, realizing what I was doing. She hit the speed dial again.

"Do you hear something?" I asked, thinking that I did. I

moved closer to the house and the old well.

"Voicemail."

"Call again."

Nothing down the well. I walked quickly toward the railroad tracks. Could I hear something now? Marge was right behind me and called again without being asked. We were about fifty feet from the railroad tracks and I could just hear parts of a song that I couldn't quite make out.

Marge dialed again. I was standing beside the half collapsed rail platform. The roof was almost completely gone, but the platform had been made out of huge twelve-inch posts and three-inch by twelve-inch planks and was mostly intact. Now I could hear it clearly. Simon and Garfunkel's "Sound of Silence" was coming from a hole where one of the planks had broken.

I got up on the platform and walked over to the broken plank. I laid down and tried to reach for the phone. I put the idea of rattlesnakes far from my mind as I stretched my arm into the hole. But it was no use. My arm was still ten inches too short.

"Stop," I told Marge, who was still dialing her brother's number. "I can't reach it." I looked around. We only had a little bit of daylight left, and I didn't see any other signs that Hank had been here. "I think we need to call in help."

Marge nodded, staring at her phone as if it could provide answers.

I called Shantel.

"You know it's past six?" she groused.

"I know," I said, trying to sound contrite. "I wouldn't ask if I didn't think it was important."

"You are really messing with me," Shantel said, sounding only mildly annoyed. "I'll be there in half an hour. Marcus has already gone home so I'll grab whoever is on shift."

Next I called dispatch and asked them to send me any deputies they could spare. They said it might be as much as an hour. The hours between five and seven were always busy for patrol as people had accidents on the way home or, once home, discovered that their house had been broken into.

While Marge and I waited, I texted Cara. She was still at the vet clinic, helping to prep for Saturday's Springtime in the Square festival. The Adams County Humane Society would be having an adoption booth and Dr. Barnhill and his staff had all volunteered to help out. Cara told me that they were putting together little flower accessories to dress up the collars and harnesses of the adoptable pets. If it weren't for how often she had to deal with the unpleasantness of sick and dying pets, I would have been a bit envious of her job.

Dill finally called me back. "No one's seen Hank since the day before yesterday. I talked with his sponsor. He said he'd check out a few places and give you a call if he finds anything."

"Thanks, Dill."

Ten minutes after I hung up with him, Shantel pulled up in the crime scene van. She had a long-handled trash picker with her that we were able to use to reach Hank's cell phone.

After Shantel pulled a couple of prints off of the phone, we checked the recent calls and text messages. An unidentified number called Hank's phone around the time that Marge had last seen him. I called Darlene and brought her up to speed before asking her to check out the number. It was probably from a burner, but you had to try.

Half an hour later we were joined by a couple of patrol deputies. By now the sun was down and we were looking for evidence by flashlight.

"We aren't going to get anywhere like this," I told Marge. "We've swept the area within a couple of hundred yards of the cell phone, but if we do any more in the dark, we're as liable to damage evidence as find it."

She thought about this for a moment before answering. "I understand. I'll start calling everyone we know. I don't think I can worry about what people think anymore." Marge was beaten down by this point.

I sealed the area as best I could with crime scene tape after everyone else had left. I assured Marge that we'd be back at the crack of dawn and widen the search as much as we needed to. She thanked me and told me she'd let me know if any friends or relatives had had contact with him.

I headed home to get a shower, feed Ivy and grab a bite to eat, but I had no intention of calling it a night. There were two people I was determined to get in contact with before going to bed—Eddie and Marcy.

CHAPTER SIXTEEN

I sent off texts to Eddie and Marcy as I ate a peanut butter and jelly sandwich with a glass of milk for dinner. I shared a bit of the milk with Ivy and told her I'd try to be a more attentive housemate in the future.

Eddie was the first to respond: *I'm busy*

Me: *Not an acceptable answer. Meet at the usual place in an hour.*

Eddie: *K*

I still hadn't received a response from Marcy by the time I met Eddie at the cemetery and told him to get in my car.

"We could just talk here," he whined.

"This isn't going to be one of our usual five-minute conversations in return for twenty dollars," I informed him. "Things are going down fast and I need every bit of information you have. Maybe even some information you don't know that you have. Understand?" With two bodies and a missing person, I was in no mood to play games.

"I hear you," he said morosely.

"I'm not sure you do. To be clear, I want a rundown on this whole stupid gold-hunting expedition."

Eddie's head snapped toward me. He was obviously surprised that I'd finally connected him to the gold, but he hid it well. "Where are we going?"

"To the office."

"No, hey, you can't. You know that I can't be seen talking to you. The trial is still a ways off. They'll kill me if they think I'm giving you any information."

Eddie was talking about the upcoming trial of his father, grandfather and half a dozen other minions of their little drug empire. Eddie had helped provide some of the information that eventually led to their arrests a couple of months ago. And he wasn't kidding about being killed if they found out that he'd be giving evidence against them in the upcoming trials.

"Don't worry." I pulled out my handcuffs and tossed them over to him. "Put those on. Behind your back. I'm bringing you in as a material witness in the murders of Hank Parrish Senior and his son, Joe Parrish."

"You're kidding, right?" Eddie asked in a very small voice.

"No, I'm not kidding. Look, this will actually make you look better if it gets back to your clan. Better for you if it looks like we occasionally harass you." I was telling him the truth, but I also wanted to shake him up. He'd become very lackadaisical about his position as CI. I needed him off balance and ready to spill his guts.

Still unsure, Eddie started the awkward procedure of putting a pair of handcuffs on behind his back in a moving vehicle. He'd managed to do it by the time I got the car parked at the office.

"Don't say a word about our CI relationship or about the case against your family. Remember, there is CCTV everywhere so assume that everything you say and do is being recorded."

"Yeah, okay." He sounded nervous and I could actually feel him shaking as I took his upper arm and led him into the building.

At night the office was pretty quiet. The front door was locked to the public, so there wasn't even a desk sergeant on duty. I took Eddie back to an interrogation room and uncuffed his hands.

Sitting across from each other, I looked into his face. Fear radiated from his eyes. I felt a little bad about this, but I knew him and I needed him to take this seriously. I didn't want to spend any more time dicking around.

"Hank Junior is missing," I told him bluntly, watching his reaction. His mouth fell open and his eyes opened wide. I knew him well enough to know that he was no actor.

"Damn!" he said.

"What do you know about his disappearance?"

"Nothin'. Like, what could I know?"

"When was the last time you saw him?"

"Like, years…" he started then stopped. "Okay, I saw him about a week ago. Just for a minute."

"Damn it, Eddie! He was one of the guys you saw Marcy with, wasn't he? Why didn't you tell me that from the beginning? Never mind… Any idea what they were talking about?"

"I couldn't hear them, but…" His voice dropped so low I could barely hear him. "I guess it had to do with… you know."

"With what?" I did know, but I wanted him to say the word.

"The…" He looked up at the camera and turned his back to it as best he could, leaning forward and continuing in a low voice, "gold."

"What gold?" I asked loudly.

He sat back. "Come on, man," he whined.

"What gold do you think they were talking about?"

Again Eddie leaned forward and hissed, "There *is* gold. Maybe a share for you too. Let up. We don't want everyone in on the treasure." He jerked his head backward toward the camera.

"Mr. Thompson, I won't mince words. There. Is. No. Gold."

"Arrrrgggh. Yes. There. Is!" He suddenly realized he'd said this at a normal volume and leaned in to whisper. "I've seen it!"

I was getting totally fed up with this whole gold hunt. "Okay. Slowly, tell me what you've seen."

"I saw a Nazi gold coin, okay. Happy?"

"Who showed you this coin?"

"Marcy. She showed it to me about a week after we got here. Hey, can you, like, destroy the footage from that camera?" he asked, pointing up at the wall.

"You're sure that it was gold?" I ignored his question about the video footage.

"Yeah, and it had an eagle and a swastika on it. That was one side. On the other was a guy."

I took out my phone, pulled up Safari and Googled: *Nazi gold coin*. After a two-minute search, I turned the phone around and let Eddie read it. The gist was that the Nazis never minted any gold coins. Some coins might have been gold-plated after the fact, but there were no Nazi gold coins.

"Well… That's what the coin looked like," Eddie mumbled.

"And you didn't take five minutes to Google it?" Of course, the answer was simple—he had *wanted* to believe in buried Nazi loot. Had Marcy been taken in too, or was she playing Eddie for the fool? I was sure that it was the former. She seemed to have drunk all the Kool-Aid about the treasure.

"Okay. We've established that there is no gold. But you believed in the legend. You think Marcy does too?"

"For sure. She was, like, we've got to find this and we're all going to be rich."

"Why did she tell you about the treasure?"

"She wanted me to check with my relatives to see if they had any information. Phillip Thompson was my granddad's brother. Marcy thought that someone in the family might have heard something. 'Sides, she said it was right that a Thompson be in on finding it since a Thompson was killed getting it off the train."

"Stealing it off the train," I corrected.

"The government stole it in the first place," he said petulantly. I didn't bother getting into the differences between a state and an individual, or the fact that just because you steal something from a thief, it doesn't make it yours. Or the fact that the theft never even happened...

I knew Marcy. She'd brought Eddie in on the deal because she wanted a flunky to do the grunt work. I looked at Eddie and thought Marcy's judgment must be getting pretty poor if she had sized Eddie up as a good prospect for a toady. Toady maybe, but a hard-working toady? Not so much. Then a thought occurred to me.

"You've got a thing for her, don't you?" I asked and his head jerked up. The look in his eyes told me everything I needed to know. *Poor Eddie*, I thought.

"Uh, no," he said unconvincingly. I let it go. Love counselor was not part of my job description. I wondered if Marcy knew about his interest in cross-dressing.

"Why is she so convinced the gold exists? Besides the gold coin?" Marcy had always been on the lookout for easy money, but she also had a pretty keen eye for a scam. Never try to scam a scammer.

"That book used to belong to her grandfather. She said there's a code or something that we can use with the book to find out where the gold is."

"Who told her about the code?"

"I don't know. I think the same person who gave her the coin," Eddie said, which made sense. Someone was pushing the gold hunt agenda, but who and why?

"Who stole the backhoe and dug those holes down by the railroad tracks?"

"I don't know. Really," he said.

"Who's Joel Patrick?" I asked and Eddie's reaction was immediate. He turned bright red and began grinding his teeth.

"You need to arrest him."

"Glad to, just tell me what he's done."

"He's been trying to horn in on the gold," Eddie said, but

I thought there might be another reason he was so anti-Joel.

"Let me guess. He likes Marcy too."

Eddie looked away, grinding his teeth the whole time, but wouldn't answer.

"Tell me more about Joel. I'll be glad to lock him up for you if you can give me just cause," I said reasonably.

"He's a crook. Drinks too much. Always flirting with Marcy. He thinks he knows where the gold is. Told Marcy she didn't need the book 'cause he had information that no one else did. But he wouldn't tell us."

I'd never seen Eddie so mad. He had it bad for Marcy.

"But I think he was lying," Eddie said and I suspected that he was right. Joel seemed as caught up in the gold fever as Marcy and Eddie. And maybe Hank? He'd been interested in the legend years ago. Was he involved with this gang that couldn't shoot straight? Maybe he was the one that was egging them on.

"Did Joel steal the truck and the backhoe?"

"Yeah, maybe."

"Does he know Hank?"

"I guess so. Whenever Joel was around Marcy, they made me leave. But…"

"But you didn't always go far."

"A couple of times I kinda hung around outside," Eddie admitted. And that's what made Eddie a useful CI—at heart he was a sneak. Maybe it was all those years as a kid, creeping around wearing women's clothes.

"And?"

"Hank came by Marcy's house when Joel was there, so they had to know each other. Right?"

"Your logic is unimpeachable. When was this?"

"I don't know. A week ago? Something like that."

A CI with a better memory would be nice, I thought. "Where's Marcy now?"

Eddie pulled out his phone and opened an app. "She's at her folk's house," he said confidently.

"Let me see that," I said, reaching out for his phone. Sure

enough, there was a red blinking dot on a map of Calhoun.

"I installed an app on her phone a week ago. It lets me see where she is."

"Marcy let you do this?"

"She doesn't know about it. Marcy's not very smart when it comes to phones and computers and stuff," he said. I looked at him with a new appreciation. He had all the makings of a professional stalker.

"I'm a little confused about the timeline and how everything fits together. From the moment that you and Marcy met, go through all the different events that got her little gold-hunting party going and then bring it up to date."

"Right. Okay. I met Marcy in the bar she was working at on South Beach. She was bartending there. Damn, she was hot behind the bar, mixing drinks, all the guys flirting with her. She has this one drink that she—"

I held up my hand to stop him. "Less about Marcy's charms and more about the gold fever."

"Anyway, we got to talking and, you know, being from the same place, that kind of bonded us. We hung out a few times and then, when her dad got sick, she wanted someone to ride up with her. I needed to get out of South Beach anyway. I was doing way too much…," he stopped himself and looked up at the camera, "…drinking, way too much drinking. So I came up here with her. Then, I don't know, we'd been up here about a week. I was crashing at her parents' house. I don't think her mom was too happy about that, but with Marcy's dad being sick, her mom was spending most of her time at the hospital or nursing home, whatever."

"The gold," I prompted

"The gold, right. Marcy said that her family and mine had a secret. There was gold that had been stolen a long time ago. I remembered hearing about it. She said that she had some information and knew a guy who might help us. Well, that turned out to be Joel. But I think someone else was involved too. Maybe it was Hank. She wouldn't tell me much. It was like she didn't trust me to keep my mouth shut." Recognizing irony was not in Eddie's wheelhouse.

"Go on."

"Not much else to tell. She talked about the book that you had. Of course, she didn't know I knew you. You know, she doesn't like you very much."

"I'm okay with that."

"We went down by the railroad tracks a couple of times and looked around. I've got a friend that works in a pawn shop in Tallahassee and he lent me a metal detector. But we didn't have much luck with that. There's, like, all kinds of metal and junk around those tracks. And when you get away from the tracks, all you find is old rusted tractor parts and crap."

"Marcy wasn't worried you all'd get caught?"

"Funny. Now that you mention it, I remember her saying that we had the Parrishes' permission, but we had to be careful not to get caught, which didn't make a lot of sense."

It made sense if you had one of the Parrishes' permission, but if not all of the family knew what you are doing. More and more, it was looking like Hank Junior was knee-deep in the hunt for gold.

Eddie chatted on a bit more, but I could tell that I'd mined all the useful information I was going to get out of him.

"Let's go." I stood up.

"Where?"

"Wherever you want for now. I'm going to go pick up Marcy. Check your app. Is she still at home?"

He pulled up the app. "Yeah."

"Good. You should probably avoid Marcy's folks' house for a couple of hours."

"You aren't going to arrest her?"

"Don't worry about it," I said and held the door open for him. He hurried out, trying to keep an eye on me, all concerned that I might lock up his girlfriend.

"Does she even know you have a thing for her?" I asked him as we walked to the front of the building.

"Yeah, maybe, I don't know."

"So you haven't told her, and you all haven't done anything."

"Not yet."

"Sad. Eddie, you've got to go for it. She's crazy as hell. Tell her you have the hots for her and if she turns you down, you win. If she says cool, you win. Either way, you win."

I followed him out the front door. On the way to my car, I pulled out my cell phone and called Darlene. "I know it's late, but I'm going to go round up Marcy."

"On my way," was her answer. I told her where I'd be and suggested that she park nearby and walk over to my car. We'd go in together.

CHAPTER SEVENTEEN

The Pikes had a nice house in an older area outside of town. Most of the houses sat on five to ten acres, so it wasn't hard to find a spot to park where I wouldn't be noticed from the house, but where Darlene could easily find me.

She arrived just a few minutes after I did. *Is she always ready to walk out the door?* I wondered.

"I don't live that far away," she said as though she'd read my mind. She got into my car. "It's the low brick house?"

"Yep. Her mother may be there, and Marcy might put up a hissy fit. You never know with her," I said as I started the car and drove the last hundred feet before pulling into their driveway behind the red car I'd seen Marcy driving. The house was surrounded by large slash pines and azaleas. The moon was full and bright enough to give the yard a silvery glow.

"Do you want to go around back or do you want me to?" I asked. On TV they love for both cops to go in the front door so there can be a big "chase the suspect" scene, but I really tried to avoid running after anyone. If you had to run, then you'd already made a mistake.

"I'll go around back," Darlene answered and headed around the side of the house.

I knocked on the door and immediately heard movement inside. The door opened and Mrs. Pike stood in the doorway. I hadn't seen her in years and it was obvious that the stress of taking care of someone who was terminally ill had taken its toll.

"Hi, Mrs. Pike. You probably don't remember me. I'm Larry Macklin. Your daughter and I dated years ago."

"Oh, yes, I'm sorry. I'm terrible with faces. Of course. Can I help you?"

"I'm an investigator with the sheriff's office now and I need to talk to…," I heard an expletive from the back of the house, "…Marcy."

"Oh, ummm, yes, come in." The poor woman had also heard the commotion and looked very confused. As I entered the house I heard a sound off to my left. I turned to see Marcy stalking toward me with Darlene right behind her.

"What the hell do you want?" she greeted me.

"She went out the sliding door," Darlene explained. "I just suggested that she didn't really want to play games." Marcy turned and glared at her. I suspected that Darlene had said some other things too, which she was too polite to repeat in front of Mrs. Pike.

"Marcy, would you rather talk here or down at the office?" I asked, trying to stay calm and non-confrontational.

"Whatever," Marcy grumbled. "I don't have anything to say anyway."

We all followed Mrs. Pike into the dining room. "Can I get you all something to drink? Coffee?" she asked.

"You don't have to give them anything, for God's sake. They're the damn police," Marcy barked at her poor mother.

"We're fine," I told Mrs. Pike, who left the room, her eyes downcast.

"So what the hell do you want?" Marcy asked again, her eye blazing.

"Why do you have to be like this? You don't even know why we're here. We just want to talk to you. Ask a few questions."

"Then get it over with already," she said.

What did I ever see in her? I asked myself. *Back then, was she really that pretty?* I shook off this assessment of my shallow dating choices and asked, "When was the last time you saw Hank Parrish Junior?"

Marcy gave me a calculating look. "I don't remember. Years ago," was the lie she came up with.

"Try again."

"That's the truth."

"Compounding the lie. Try again."

"What's the point of asking me questions if you aren't going to believe my answers?" she threw back.

"What's the point of lying if the person you're lying to knows you're lying?" I lobbed back into her court.

Marcy clenched her mouth shut like a kid refusing to eat.

"Fine. I'll make it easier for you. We know that you've been seeing him off and on since you got back in town. Furthermore, I suspect that he roped you into this crazy gold-hunting scheme. Or did you rope him into it?"

"I didn't rope him into anything."

"But you now admit that you have seen him recently."

"No."

"That wasn't a question. You know, I actually admire your technique. You're managing to get information out of me without divulging anything. Here, I'll give you something else. He's gone missing."

Marcy's eyes narrowed as she tried to decide whether I was trying to trick her. She seemed to have become even more paranoid over the last couple of days.

"Two people are dead and now Hank is missing. You might want to start helping us. You are in real danger of becoming either a victim or a suspect."

I could tell that Marcy really, really wanted to spit in my face. But she controlled herself and finally answered, "I saw him a couple of days ago."

"Where did you see him?"

"Here."

"He came here?"

"No, I kidnapped him. What the hell do you think?" She had a point.

"Why did he come here?"

"None of your business."

"Which means it was about the gold. What was his involvement in your treasure hunt?"

I could see her mind working, turning over all the different answers she could give. Marcy approached lying like a chess player, calculating all the different ramifications of each lie that she could tell, and trying to decide which one would give her the best advantage.

"He owned the land." Not strictly true, but I could see why she might have needed him because of his relationship to the property. "I didn't make him do anything. He's been hunting the gold a lot longer than me."

I had to pay close attention now. When Marcy appeared to be telling the truth was when you had to be the most cautious.

"The last time you saw him, what was his mood?"

"He was real upset about his brother's murder. He kept saying that he didn't know who would do that to Joe. When I tried to talk to him about the gold, he didn't seem that interested." Marcy seemed puzzled by that. "Finally he said that he thought we were on the right track for finding out where it was buried."

"Who told you about the book and the code?"

She hesitated. "Hank. He called me right after I came back to town. Said he had information about the Nazi gold. I didn't know what he was talking about at first. He kept calling, saying that I needed to get a book that had been sent to my grandfather while he was in jail. If I got the book, then he had the code and we could put them together and find the gold."

"Did he say where he got the code?"

"He said it was in a letter he found that my grandfather had written to one of his friends."

"Where is the code now?" As soon as I said that, Marcy started to heat up.

"I don't know! I haven't seen Hank since I got the book. If you had given me the damn book the first time I asked for my stuff, we'd have already found the gold. But now I have the book and I can't find Hank." She was getting madder and madder as she went on.

"How do I know *you* don't have the code?" Marcy demanded, going into paranoia overload. "You're after the gold! That's why you keep asking me all these questions. Damn you! You aren't getting it. None of it!"

She was shrieking so loudly that her mother came back and looked into the room. As soon as Mrs. Pike saw that Darlene and I weren't killing her daughter, she sighed and left. I can only imagine that she had been watching her daughter throw tantrums for her entire life. I was impressed that she even bothered to check.

"We couldn't care less about the gold. We're trying to catch whoever murdered Hank Senior and Joe. More importantly, right now we're trying to find Hank Junior. That's all we want to do," I tried to explain.

"And what about you?" Marcy stopped and turned on Darlene. Darlene's body stiffened, ready to explode into action.

"Back off," Darlene said, unwilling to engage Marcy in conversation.

"What's wrong? I hit a nerve?"

"You will back off." No threat. Not even an order. Just a statement in a loud clear voice. With Marcy still in her personal space, Darlene rose from her chair. Darlene had an inch or two on Marcy and eyes that never wavered. Marcy held Darlene's gaze for another couple of seconds, just to save face, but there was no doubt she'd lost the stare-down contest.

"I don't care about any gold," Darlene said, still standing and carefully watching Marcy. "You need to tell us everything you know about Hank Junior, and what might have happened to him."

Marcy seemed smaller under Darlene's gaze. "I told you what I know. He was here. We talked about… his brother dying, and the gold, and then he left."

"You have no idea what might have happened to him?"

Marcy didn't say anything for a few minutes. Maybe she realized that finding Hank was as important to her as it was to us. Without Hank, she had no chance of finding the gold.

"He seemed… Look, I've been pretty strung out before, and I've seen addicts that have been clean for a while, but fall off the wagon. That's how he was. Like a guy who's slipping. Letting go of his recovery." This was the most sincere I'd ever seen Marcy.

"What about Joel. Has he seen Hank?"

"I don't know," Marcy said. She'd gone from screaming maniac to sullen child in a matter of minutes. I wondered if a doctor had ever slapped a bi-polar label on her.

"Where is Joel?"

"I guess at the motel."

"Okay, we're leaving. If you think of anything else call… Deputy Marks." Both Marcy and Darlene gave me dirty looks, but Darlene took out one of her cards and held it out to Marcy who, reluctantly, accepted it.

Outside, I turned to Darlene. "Let's swing by the motel."

Darlene followed me to the motel, where we found Joel. Predictably, he didn't know anything about Hank's disappearance. I reminded him again about not leaving town, then headed home for some much needed sleep.

CHAPTER EIGHTEEN

Dawn came early. I was up and out to the Parrishes' property before the sun was fully over the horizon. Damn if Darlene wasn't already there waiting for me.

We spread out a geological survey map on the hood of my car. "If he's still around here, he might have wandered off onto Florida Pines land," Darlene said.

About a hundred yards on the other side of the railroad tracks was the beginning of a huge track of land owned by the Florida Pines timber company. The property was designated as a wildlife management area and covered almost ten thousand acres. Divided into parcels that were timbered for pulp wood on rotation, the area was crisscrossed by dozens of dirt logging roads. Some parts were covered in twenty-year slash pines while others had been clear-cut this past summer.

"Of course, he might have been picked up by someone and not be anywhere around here," I said.

"We don't have much choice. We have to make the effort to search the area until we have information that points in some other direction."

I called the watch commander and he promised to send me two deputies as soon as the morning rush was over, then

I checked in with Marge. She hadn't heard anything new. She was busy organizing a group of farm employees, friends and family, including Clive and Jane, to help with the search and she said they'd be there soon. All pretense of keeping this within the family had gone out the window.

By nine o'clock we had everyone briefed and as organized as we were going to get. We fanned out to the south and east, away from the Parrish property. After only half an hour, Deputy Sykes found a sweatshirt and a jeweler's bag. The bag tested positive for meth. I bagged the shirt and Darlene volunteered to take it up to Hank's apartment and compare it to the other shirts in his wardrobe.

Dad pulled up just as Darlene was getting back. She came over to where I was filling him in on the search. "Sorry to interrupt, but this is a very close match for a couple of sweatshirts in his closet. Same size, about the same amount of wear. The tags are identical."

"Thanks, Darlene," I said and she headed back out to rejoin the search.

"I called over to Leon County and two of their K-9 teams should be here soon. And they've offered air support if we need it. I've also got the mounted posse on standby, depending on what the dogs find," Dad said.

"That'll help," I said.

"So what do you think really happened?"

"Honestly, it looks like Hank might have fallen completely off the wagon. Meth, and maybe heroin, but he's been known to use just about anything that would make him high or, for that matter, low. He was pretty much an equal-opportunity abuser when he was off the leash. Heroin was his favorite, but…" I shrugged. "Having been clean for a few months, he could have misjudged his tolerance."

"Yeah, that's not uncommon." Dad nodded.

"Then, in an impaired state and with his fixation on finding this stupid lost gold, he could have easily convinced himself that he was on the trail of something and wandered who knows where into these woods. On the other hand, that might be what he, or someone else, wants us to believe. Maybe the dogs can put us on the right track," I said and Dad nodded grimly.

"I hate election years. I'm always second-guessing myself. Am I doing all of this because of who Hank is or, should I say, who his family is? Probably. We have families calling in every day about their kids, drug addicts that have gone missing. We file a report and put out a bulletin, but we don't call out the National Guard," Dad mused.

"Be fair. This man is also a suspect in a pair of murders. Not only is he a suspect, but his relationship to the earlier victims puts him at high risk of being murdered himself."

Dad put his hand on my shoulder. "Thanks. I'll be back in touch later. I'll leave it to you and Marks to coordinate everything here."

When Dad called at noon, I was able to report on the work of the K-9 teams. "Dogs got here about an hour ago. They followed the trail from where the shirt was found to Sandy Bottom Creek. The handlers thought they picked up a couple of trails on the other side of the creek, but they couldn't be sure. They did find some footprints in the creek bed that are probably Hank's."

"That would have him moving deeper onto Florida Pines land."

"Afraid so."

"I called over there earlier, just to let them know what was going on. They don't have any objections to us searching their land. In fact, they said they'd send one of their crews out to help. I'll call Bob and have him bring out the posse, then I'll get the boys and join you down there."

By "the boys," Dad meant Finn and Mac, his two old-style American Quarter Horses. In the past I'd resisted Dad's penchant for throwing me up on Mac every chance he got as part of the mounted posse, but today I was looking forward to it. The Parrishes and some of their neighbors had brought down their ATVs, but even those vehicles couldn't go everywhere a horse could. I was tired of walking from search group to search group. Being mounted would be a real advantage, with a better line of sight and the ability to cover more ground in less time.

Darlene had commandeered one of the four-wheelers and was buzzing around, following up on anything that the searchers found. The woods were full of a hundred years' worth of farming and hunting cast-offs. Most of it was obviously irrelevant, but we told the searchers to report anything they found. Before anything could be discarded, either a crime scene tech, Darlene or myself had to put eyes on it.

Bob Muller showed up just before two with a couple of horse trailers and five members of the mounted posse. Bob was a retired deputy who put his heart and soul into the posse. The department had bought two used horse trailers for the posse to use, and Bob meticulously maintained them and all of the posse's equipment. Bob rode an older Saddlebred that he loved for its easy gait.

I showed Bob a map of the area and indicated the best places for the posse to start—areas where the pines were mature and the ground was thick with palmettos.

As the posse headed out, Dad drove up with his horse trailer, followed by Jamie, Mauser's dog-sitter, and the big dog himself. They had brought a pop-up tent to serve as a refreshment and first aid station. The fire department was on its way with ice, food and medical supplies. We were lucky that the weather was cool, but we were already getting some volunteers that had pushed themselves too hard. I recruited a couple of folks to help Jamie set up the tent, then helped Dad unload the horses. As usual, Finn was lively and curious while his brother Mac dozed off while I brushed him down.

Saddled and mounted, Dad and I headed out to check in with the search groups.

"Why'd you bring Mauser?" I asked. Not that Dad wasn't willing to bring Mauser to just about any function, but I was still a bit surprised.

"Jamie wanted to do something, so I figured he could

help with the refreshments. And, when I got to thinking about it, Mauser will be a bit of comic relief for everyone."

Maybe he was right. I'd been on a couple of other search and rescue operations, and most of the time was spent searching rather than rescuing. It was easy to become fatigued and disillusioned.

At six o'clock, with the sun beginning to slip behind the trees, Dad and I returned to search HQ. We were done for the day. Having search parties out at night would only end up compounding our problems.

As I dismounted, I realized that it had been a while since I'd spent more than an hour or two on horseback. I was feeling sore in muscles that I didn't even know I had. I tied Mac to the posse's picket line and took off his saddle, then walked over to the refreshment tent. There I found Jamie handing out bottled water and chips while Mauser reclined on the ground, allowing people to pet and admire him. When he saw me, he stood up and came lumbering over to beat me with his tail and slobber on my clothes.

"Yeah, you big lazy dog. You didn't even get off of your bed at the office the other day."

Mauser ignored my ridicule and leaned hard into me. I scratched him until my arms were sore, then pushed him off on a young fireman named Jerry who couldn't believe how big the dog was.

I was guzzling a bottle of water when Darlene came over. She was covered in dust, but other than that looked like she'd just stepped out of the office.

"Nothing. I figure we've covered a couple hundred acres pretty thoroughly. Leon's helicopter was able to cover all of the clear-cut areas, so we can mark them as being searched. Level one, of course," she reported.

We had agreed on three levels for the search. Level one was eyeballs from a distance, like a plane or helicopter. Level two was searched on foot or from horseback with a density of about five people per acre. Level three was an intense search for any evidence. We'd done a level three search within two hundred yards of where Hank's phone was found.

I looked over to see Jerry playing with Mauser. He was crouched down, mock wrestling with the giant dog like you would a Boxer or a Pitbull.

"I wouldn't do that if I was you," I said to him as a good-natured warning.

He looked at me the way firemen have always looked at cops, as if to say, *You guys aren't tough enough.* "Don't worry, I've got a big 'ol Rottweiler at home," Jerry said with a boyish grin.

With perfect timing, Mauser chose that moment to jump up and punch Jerry right in the eye with one of his ten-pound paws, knocking him to the ground. Mauser followed up the blow by jumping up and down on top of the fireman, who was mumbling a few choice words as he rolled right and left, trying to get out from under the playful and delighted Great Dane.

I snapped a leash on Mauser's collar while Jamie ran over to help Jerry up off the ground.

"Big guy, you play too rough," Jerry said. But, in a true show of sportsmanship, he bent down and gave Mauser a good scratching to show that there were no hard feelings.

On Wednesday morning the weather unleashed a seasonal downpour that soon settled into a steady drizzle, so we started out with only the hardcore volunteers and professionals. Jane, Marge and Clive were there, but the strain on the family was beginning to show. Several times I caught them bickering about directions, or when to take a break. They were also still trying to figure out the funeral details. They'd decided to have Hank's and Joe's burials at the same time, but now they couldn't decide how long to wait with Hank Junior missing.

Cara took the morning off and braved the weather to ride with me. I let her ride Mac while I took the hyperactive Finn.

It would have been very romantic riding through the pine woods with her if we hadn't been hunting for a dead body in the rain.

We were soaked to the bone by noon and my legs were chaffed from riding a wet horse. Cara threw in the towel and left for work while I took a break at the refreshment tent. Darlene drove up on her ATV as I was contemplating the water dripping off of my hat.

"This is frustrating as hell," I said.

"I hear you, partner," Darlene said in her best cowboy drawl. I was impressed that she was able to keep a sense of humor under these conditions.

"Any ideas?" I asked her.

"We need to keep it up the rest of the day. Have half the crews continue expanding the search grid and bring the other half back in and start them from the center to re-search the area closest to the point where the phone was recovered," she suggested.

"You think we missed something?"

"I think it's possible."

"You have a point. I've certainly heard about cases where the body was found in an area that had been searched once."

"Then we're agreed that we're looking for a body at this point?"

"If he's in the woods, yes. I still think there's a good chance that this is all a giant red herring and he's off doing drugs with some meth-addicted skank," I said brutally, my exhaustion getting the best of me.

"If that's the case, then we'll present the family with a bill and then kill him," Darlene said, wiping the rain out of her eyes.

I laughed in spite of myself. "Agreed. We also need to go over Hank's apartment with a fine-toothed comb. Will you ask Shantel and Marcus to schedule some time for that?"

"Now you're thinking," she said before driving off again.

CHAPTER NINETEEN

The rain stopped by one o'clock and a few more volunteers showed up. After making sure they all had assignments, I convinced myself to climb back up on Mac, even though every muscle in my body told me that it was a really bad idea. Holding the reins, I saw another car pull up. My old partner Pete clambered out of the driver's side while his youngest daughter, Kim, hopped out of the other.

"Am I too late to rent an ATV?" Pete asked. He was wearing old BDUs, a flannel shirt and work boots.

"Sorry, they've all been taken." I reached down and shook his hand.

"What's his name?" Kim asked me, petting Mac's nose.

I answered her, watching as Mac's eyelids went to half mast and his head lowered to give the girl full access to his nose. "How'd your dad talk you into coming out in the woods?"

"I want to help," Kim said. She was in jeans, a flannel shirt and rubber boots.

"Grab your jacket," Pete told her and she trotted back to the car. "She's my tomboy. Crazy girl thinks she wants to be a cop. Of course, Jenny wanted to spend time with me too until she discovered boys."

Kim rejoined us, wearing a pink quilted jacket.

"You all can man the refreshment tent," I suggested, knowing that Pete wasn't fond of traipsing through the woods. After his "hard work" yesterday, Mauser had refused to leave the house with Jamie that morning, so we had been leaving the tent unmanned.

"I want to search," Kim stated firmly. Pete rolled his eyes.

"I've got a group searching about half a mile to the north. You can just follow this logging road out to them," I suggested, pointing to a muddy track heading off through the piney woods.

"You're sure there isn't a spare four-wheeler?" Pete grumbled.

"Mom says you need to exercise more." Kim playfully punched him in the gut.

"Ugggh, no fair ganging up on me. Okay, okay," Pete said, laughing. "I've got my radio," he said to me, tapping the handheld set on his belt.

"Let's go," Kim said and began trotting down the muddy road.

"Lord help me," Pete said and started after her.

I rode down another road to check on the Parrishes, who had formed a search party made up of themselves and a dozen employees. I'd just ridden up to Marge when I heard Pete's voice, pitched higher than normal, coming over my radio.

"I think we have your man," he said.

"Come back?"

"I'm at a culvert on the logging road about a quarter mile from the camp. You'll need to get the coroner," he answered, his voice tense. I realized that finding a body with his daughter might not qualify as a fun family outing.

"Roger that. I'm on my way."

Marge had heard the transmission. She put her hand over her mouth and stifled a cry.

"I'm going to check it out. Continue searching. This

might be nothing. And I wouldn't say anything to anyone else yet," I told her. I knew that if Pete said he found a body, then he'd found a body. But I didn't want the whole family rushing to the scene. Marge nodded her head.

Sensing my urgency, Mac consented to a brisk trot. When we came around a bend about a hundred feet from the culvert, I could see Pete standing there with his arm around his daughter, holding her close to his side.

I brought Mac to a halt in front of them. Dismounting, I asked Kim if she'd hold the horse while her dad and I checked things out. She nodded and took the reins, holding them the way I showed her.

"I'll take care of him," she said, sounding younger and more vulnerable than she had half an hour earlier.

Once we were far enough away, Pete said, "Not pretty. When we came down the road there was a buzzard sitting on the edge of the culvert. Kim pointed it out. I told her that there was probably a dead animal inside, but she insisted on checking it out. Thank you, God, that I took the flashlight and looked in the pipe first."

We stopped and looked down at the culvert. The pipe ran under the road, providing a way for water to pass from one side of the road to the other. The land on both sides of the road was low, with sweetgum trees and red maples intermixed with magnolias and pines. The rain this morning hadn't been enough to fill the ditch on either side of the road, but the ground was muddy.

"That's not very big," I said skeptically. The corrugated pipe that ran under the road couldn't have been more than eighteen inches wide.

"Trust me," Pete said. "Can't you smell it?"

He was right about the odor, but I still couldn't believe that Hank Junior was in that pipe. "Hank is a big guy," I said.

"Yeah, okay. I don't know for sure that it's Hank, but believe me, there is a dead guy stuffed in that pipe. Do you want to see the front end or the back end?" Pete asked, pointing to the east side of the road for the head and the west side for the feet.

"I guess I'll take the head," I said, taking Pete's flashlight and making my way down to the ditch.

"Not sure that's the best choice," Pete said critically.

The odor of rotting flesh was much stronger down there. Bending down and peering in, I couldn't see anything inside the small dark pipe. I turned on the flashlight and, trying to hold my breath, got down on my hands and knees in the mud.

I shined the light into the culvert pipe and gasped involuntarily. Staring back at me were the cloudy white eyes of a corpse. From the hair and general appearance, I was pretty sure that it was Hank, but under those conditions it was difficult to be sure. The body looked like it was wedged in solid. I got up and went around to the other side of the road. On my way, I looked over to where Kim was trying to feed Mac wiregrass. "I'm really glad she didn't see that," I told Pete as I passed him.

Looking from the other side of the pipe, the feet were a lot closer to me than the head had been. If I'd reached in, I could have touched his shoes.

I walked downwind from the culvert and called Dr. Darzi. "And don't send the hired help. I think this is going to require the boss onsite," I told him.

I also called Marge and informed her that the search was over. I told her to take the rest of the family back up to the house and that we'd come meet with them as soon as we could.

Forty-five minutes later, Dr. Darzi, Pete, Darlene and I were standing around discussing how to proceed. "You are simply going to have to dig up the pipe," Darzi told us, shaking his head. "He has bloated. The only way to get the body out without damaging it and destroying evidence will be to cut the pipe off of him."

All of us were quiet for a few moments, then I pulled out my phone and called Dad. I explained what we had found and he offered to call Florida Pines and give them an update.

"Who do you want me to call to dig out the pipe?" I asked.

"Good question. Only three months into the new year and we're running through money like water. Damn it, I guess we don't have time to take bids. Okay, call Crawley's Land Clearing. I know they have the equipment to do it. Just try to talk them down on the price. I'll be down soon to pick up the horses," he said and hung up.

Small county, small budget. Luckily, old man Crawley decided that he could eat off of this story for years to come and offered to do it for cost.

After the backhoe uncovered the pipe, we were able to use it, and the assistance of a dozen men, to lift the pipe out and set it on the back of a flatbed pickup truck. Darzi sealed the ends of the pipe as best he could, and I made absolutely sure that the thing was strapped down tight. It was completely dark by the time we finished.

"I've already checked with the hospital and they have someone who can cut it open," Dr. Darzi said. "I'll do the autopsy as soon as we've cracked the shell and gotten your nut out." He chuckled darkly, but with the corpses piling up, I didn't find his joke very funny.

"Do you think he got in there on his own or was someone able to push the body inside?" I asked.

"My opinion, based just on what I've seen, is that he crawled in there on his own. I don't think that anyone could have pushed a body as big as you say he was up into that pipe. Force him to crawl in there…? Maybe. But more likely, a severe mental breakdown, possibly fueled by drugs, led him to crawl in there on his own," Darzi said as the truck carrying the pipe drove off down the dirt road. "But I'll know a lot more after I've seen the body and we have a toxicology report." He got into his car and followed his latest science experiment back to the morgue.

"We better go talk to the family," I said to Darlene.

"This is going to be tough," Darlene said in a classic understatement as we parked in front of the main house.

"Let's get it over with."

I knocked on the door and once again we were ushered into their inner sanctum to tell them how another member of their family had been killed.

"Are you telling me that you still don't have any idea who's doing this?" Clive's face was bright red and his eyes were literally bulging with suppressed emotion.

"Yes." I wished I had a different answer, but what else could I say?

"Who's going to be next?" Clive started to get out of his chair, but Marge put her hand on his arm. Without even looking at her, he settled back down.

"We don't know what killed Hank. There is a strong possibility that he was high on drugs…"

"But you don't know that!" Marge interrupted. Jane rolled her eyes and Andrew huffed.

"No, we don't. But intoxication could have contributed to his death. However, we have to go with the assumption that others in the family might be in danger. One of the things I'd advise is for you all to stay together. Skip anything that you do routinely."

"What?" Jane asked.

"If someone is stalking your family, the worst thing you can do is remain predictable," Darlene explained.

"That's ridiculous. If someone is stalking us, then you need to protect us," Andrew said, using his outdoor voice.

"We can't protect you 24/7," I said calmly. "But we're going to be working to catch the person who's committed these crimes. One of the best ways you all can help us is by giving us information."

Andrew threw up his hands. "You've already questioned us. Twice! We've told you what we know. This is some sick serial killer who's chosen to pick on our family."

I really wanted to tell him that he wasn't officially a part of this family, so why didn't he wait outside, but I didn't think that would fly. Instead I said, "Random murder is unlikely. We believe…," I looked at Darlene for support and she gave a slight nod, "…that the killer has targeted you all for a very specific motive."

"What motive?" Jane asked.

"If we knew the motive we'd probably know the killer," I said. "Money, revenge or something more cryptic. But the odds are that the murderer is someone who one or all of you know or have known in the past. So please think. Run past events over in your head. Look for someone who might have a reason to want to hurt your father and your brother. Maybe both your brothers."

I was doing my best, but all I was getting were sullen looks, and who could blame them? The family was being picked off one by one and we weren't any closer to finding the person responsible.

"What about this Joel guy?" Clive suggested and got a look from Jane and Marge. "What?" he asked them.

"I really don't think that an old boyfriend of mine is seeking revenge. Even I would admit that I wasn't *that* hot," Jane said.

"Well, we know he's in town," Clive insisted.

"I've seen him a couple of times," Jane admitted.

"A couple times? You told us about seeing him when you were driving. What other time did you see him?" I inquired.

Jane looked at me as though she'd forgotten I was in the room. "Oh, well, a week ago, I guess. I just passed him in the Supersave." I didn't believe that she ever went inside the Supersave, but now was not the time to confront her about it. I just filed it away.

"When can we have the funeral?" Marge asked. She always reverted to the practical matters at hand.

"Are we still having all the funerals together? I mean, are we including Hank in the funeral with Dad and Joe?" Jane asked.

"We'd better or there won't be anyone at his," Andrew

said, receiving my Heartless Bastard of the Year award.

"I think it would be the right thing to do," Marge said, giving Andrew an ice cold stare. He started to roll his eyes and thought better of it.

"I can't say for sure when Hank's body will be released. I would think that Marshall's Funeral Home should be able to pick… him up by Friday." I tried to put it as delicately as possible.

"Poor Daddy has already waited a week," Jane said. "But it wouldn't be fair not to include Hank Junior."

"I agree. I couldn't go through two funerals. We'll bury all three at the same time. I'll talk to Mr. Marshall first thing in the morning," Marge said. Clive reached over and put his arm around her shoulder. Andrew must have thought it was a contest, because he reached out and took Jane's hand.

The worst of it was over. Darlene and I asked a few more questions, but it was clear that the family had reached their emotional limit. Pressing them further wasn't going to get us any answers tonight.

After two grueling days in the woods and all of the anxiety of a murder investigation stuck in neutral, I was glad to come home to a warm meal. Cara had texted earlier that she was going over to my place and would have dinner ready for me whenever I got there.

I managed to drag myself through the front door just before ten o'clock. The aroma of garlic, tomatoes and sausage was welcome. I hadn't eaten a proper meal since Hank went missing.

"Lasagna," Cara said after giving me a hug. "Go get a hot shower and I'll get everything on the table."

"You're too good to me."

"Don't get too used to it. I'm on my best behavior," she told me with a smile that made me feel even better. A relationship without some good-natured kidding would be torture.

I might not have felt like a new man after the shower and dinner, but I felt less like I'd been in a two-day boxing match. I sat down at the table and plowed into my meal.

"So what are you going to do now?" Cara asked.

"Depends on what we find out from the autopsy. Regardless, I think we're going to have to put the spotlight on the family."

"And the gold hunters."

"Wildcards. The gold hunt definitely has ties to the family, but I just don't see either Marcy or Joel committing murder for it. And now that Hank is gone… Darlene and I are just going to have to comb through the evidence again and see if we can come up with something that points us in the right direction."

Tomorrow was St. Patrick's Day so, in a nod to the Celtic side of her heritage, Cara put on a Loreena McKennitt playlist. The soothing melodies made my eyelids droop. Cara took the dishes into the kitchen to wash them and I'm pretty sure I was asleep on the couch before she even turned the water on.

CHAPTER TWENTY

On Thursday, Darlene and I went straight into the conference room to spread everything out and look at the suspects and evidence anew.

"I've found a few tidbits," Darlene said after a while, holding up a handful of printouts. "Jane and Andrew are stretched pretty thin. She's been helping him financially while he's trying to start his own law firm."

"How thin?"

"Between student loans, mortgages, car loans and credit cards, they're about five-hundred thousand in debit."

"Wow. But with student loans and mortgages these days, that's not beyond the pale. He's a lawyer and she's a paralegal, so they have the potential to stay afloat. But money could certainly be a motive for them."

"Yes, but it's not like the farm has been making a fortune either. I was talking to Bud down at the bank, and his feeling is that they aren't big enough to be really profitable. They make a good living when the weather cooperates, but that doesn't always happen."

"What's the bottom line?"

"The value of the land and equipment puts them in the black to the tune of about two million dollars. But Bud explained that that would require liquefying all the assets, including the house. Interestingly, Joe had talked to him about doing just that. Bud said he wasn't going to sell the main house, but he wanted to know how much they could get out of the rest of it. Seemed he wasn't as keen on farming as his dad was."

"Pete told me there were some rumors going around that Hank Senior was having some memory problems. I'll check with his doctor and see if he was just getting old, or if it was a sign of something more ominous," I said.

"Shantel said they're still waiting on the DNA results for the skin on the alligator."

"Hopefully it's a good sample. Though it may not do us much good since everybody in the family would share the same markers. Speaking of family, what about Marge?"

"She loves that farm. She and Clive took out a mortgage on their house to help the farm a couple of years ago when we had a dry summer. Financially, they're doing okay. At least no worse off than most Americans."

"Marge is devoted to the farm. I wonder what she'd do if she knew that Joe had talked about selling out? There's a case for her. If their dad was developing Alzheimer's or dementia and would be turning things over to Joe, and she discovered Joe wanted to sell out, she could have humanely put her dad down and then took out Joe." It was a testament to how frustrating the case was that I didn't think this was a completely ridiculous suggestion.

"I guess it's foolish to ask if she can shoot a crossbow."

"Everyone in that family started hunting when they were old enough to walk. There are a dozen pictures in the house of them with trophy bucks. But that does bring up the question of where the crossbow came from."

"Not much there. We found a couple on the property, but that doesn't do us much good. Ballistics can't match anything from a crossbow to the bolt that killed him. The bolt was a cheap and readily available brand. The closest Walmart on our side of Leon County sells them. Marcus is taking the lead on that. He emailed pictures to the company that makes them, but they're in China. The poorly translated reply said that they would probably be able to identify the year and the factory it came from, but that's about all."

"Investigations in the modern world… some things are easier while some are a lot more complicated. Okay, that brings us to our gold diggers."

"What a bunch of losers." Darlene sighed. "All of them have arrests for various offenses. We'll start with your girlfriend." She gave me a *What were you thinking?* look.

"Ex. Ex-girlfriend."

"If that helps you sleep at night. Your ex-girlfriend has a record that goes from minor driving infractions to a DUI, and from there to a bad check and an assault charge for hitting a patron in a bar."

"We know she's unstable. Marcy is absolutely capable of going too far. I would not be surprised if she accidently killed someone. On purpose though? She'd have to have a good motive. Did she kill Hank Senior because he was going to kick them off his property? That seems a little over the top. Maybe she pointed the crossbow at him and accidentally pulled the trigger. That's possible. Then Joe found out and so she had to kill him? And Hank Junior might or might not have been the victim of murder. Which reminds me, Darzi has scheduled the autopsy for noon."

"We have Joel Patrick next. He's a little piece of work himself. Fraud seems to be his favorite pastime. Many arrests and two convictions. His scams mostly run right along the thin edge between legal stealing and the illegal kind. As far as violence goes, he's usually on the receiving end. He scams someone then they get mad and attempt to break his face, is the usual pattern."

"With him, we at least have a history. He did have a physical altercation with Hank Senior."

"Yeah, but for this crumb that's the norm. A month seldom goes by that someone doesn't want to take a shot at him."

"Same scenario that we laid out for Marcy could be true for him."

"That's true. Also, if they *did* find gold, then I can imagine him fighting to defend his share, à la *The Treasure of the Sierra Madre*."

"Argggh! There is no gold! Though that does beg the question of how the whole gold hunt thing got started. Is that part of the plot or just a weird side note?"

"On to number three, Eddie Thompson. Related to the notorious Thompsons. Mostly some moving violations and a couple minor drug infractions. But considering who his father and grandfather are, I think it is safe to say that he could find it in himself to do some serious violence. However, he seems like a junior player, brought in by Marcy as her toady," Darlene finished.

I had to admire her summation of Eddie and his role, though I doubted that he could have had anything to do with the murders. I'd seen him when he was confronted by serious crimes. He got very nervous very quickly. I didn't see any of that in him now.

"Of course, there is always the other option—person or persons unknown," I threw on the table.

"We can't rule it out. But to kill two grown men, possibly three, would require a motive. I haven't seen anyone outside of our two groups with a decent motive," Darlene stated.

"I have to agree. I talked to Pete, the man with his ear to the tracks, and he hasn't heard of anything else from the breakfast set."

Until recently, Pete had eaten at Winston's Grill every morning while listening to all of the morning gossip from the local farmers and businessmen. Now, with the grill shut down, they'd had to improvise a new routine at the Donut Hole. The Hole had moved in some more chairs and built covered seating outdoors, but the morning crowd was definitely having to compromise.

"Nothing?"

"Just some typical grumblings over minor business

disputes. Parrish Farm is a big operation so you'd expect there to be a few issues. Al Parkston was having a minor tiff with Hank Senior over the lease on one of Al's fields. But none of it suggests a motive for murder."

I looked at my watch. "I don't see any reason for both of us to go to the autopsy. One of us can run over there while the other follows up on the trace evidence."

"I've got some things I can do in Tallahassee. I'll take the autopsy," Darlene said.

"Deal." I'd seen enough bad-looking corpses lately. Darlene was welcome to this one. I felt bad for the family. They'd be looking at one open and two closed caskets at the funeral. Even so, half the people who came up to pay their respects to Hank Senior would be looking to see if they could tell where the crossbow bolt went into his skull.

I went back to the area that Shantel and Marcus called home. The crime scene techs all shared the duty of storing and keeping track of evidence. As well as keeping most things under lock and key, their office and the storage rooms in the back were the most heavily monitored areas in the building, with cameras covering every inch of the space. No one wanted the department to face a chain of custody or tampering issue in the middle of a trial.

Shantel was at her computer checking email when I came in. "Look at you. How many bodies have you racked up in the last couple of weeks?" she kidded me.

"Don't remind me. Have you come up with anything useful?" I asked hopefully.

"You expect me to pull your chestnuts out of the fire?" She paused for just a second and then added, "I guess I do owe you."

"You don't owe me a thing. Speaking of what you don't owe me, how is Tonya doing?"

"Better. Fewer nightmares. Thinks the sun rises and falls with you and Pete. Poor, deluded child." Shantel smiled. "She's thinking about going into nursing. She's signed up for classes again for the spring semester at Tallahassee

Community College."

"Glad to hear she's doing better."

"I just poked the lab again. They could have our DNA from the alligator done. It just depends on where we are in the queue. Maybe later today or tomorrow. I actually got a partial fingerprint off of the bolt, but I don't think it's large enough to do much good. And we searched Hank Junior's room yesterday, but we didn't find much there either."

"Some good news, please."

"There isn't any. I did finally get in touch with the blood splatter expert and he confirmed Darzi's suspicions that there was another weapon used in the initial attack on Joe. Something light enough to swing. But he's still got to do some experiments to determine which way the object was swung and how tall the attacker probably was, etc. I'm telling you, those guys love to do their little tests. He was so excited about slinging blood around, I thought he was going to start giggling." Shantel shook her head.

"Let's do another search of Joe's house to make sure we didn't miss anything that might have been used. Have your blood expert give you a range of sizes that would match the smaller weapon."

"He pretty much said that from what he knows now, it could be anything from a golf club to a two-by-four. I'll take our new intern over and have her go through the house with me. She needs the experience. Someday I want us to have enough money to only hire experienced help. I swear I spend most of my time training people."

I left Shantel still mumbling about not getting good help.

Darlene called at three o'clock.

"You missed out on a fun one," she told me. "Darzi figures Hank was in there almost the whole time he was missing." Not a surprise. "He probably died from exposure after passing out from whatever drugs were in his system. There were no wounds or internal damage to the body, so

Darzi figures that Hank did crawl into the pipe on his own. He's ordered the toxicology lab to do a wide spectrum analysis on the blood and organ samples, which he made a point of saying is very expensive. We'll know more when the report comes back."

"Thanks for taking one for the team," I said in the spirit of comradery. I filled her in on what Shantel had told me. "Did you ask him when Marshall's could pick up the body?"

"Anytime from this afternoon on," Darlene said.

"I'll call the family."

I spent most of the afternoon on the phone. First I called Marge, who was relieved that they could move forward with the funeral preparations. I asked her to let me know when the viewing and the funeral would be. Next I briefed Lt. Johnson, my immediate supervisor, on the status of the investigation. Johnson had been in the military for twenty years and had a soldier's aversion to politics. He seemed to count his lucky stars when the sheriff stepped in on high profile cases such as these, but he and I still pretended that he was in charge.

I started to call Dad, then figured that I might as well walk the hundred feet to his office. He was on the phone, but he nodded for me to sit down. He was making small talk and, after a couple of minutes, it was obvious to me that he was reaching out to one of his political supporters. I checked to make sure that he was on his personal phone. Dad was meticulous about separating political activities from his official duties, but it wasn't like he could confine them to particular hours of the day. He just tried to make sure that he didn't use county resources.

He finally hung up after ten minutes, looking frustrated. "Do you know how much I'm going to have to spend on this election?" he asked me.

"Fifty thousand?" I tossed out.

"Maybe close to that. If Maxwell hadn't gotten into the race..." He let the sentence drift off.

I gave Dad all of the current details on the investigation.

He leaned back and listened intently. With most people, if they lean forward it's a sign that they are engaged and paying attention. But I'd learned as a kid that when Dad really wanted to concentrate on what you were saying, he'd lean back and half close his eyes. I figured out that he was trying to let his mind hear the words rather than let his eyes focus on things that would distract him from what you were saying. However, if he was trying to gauge a person's honesty, then he'd aim both headlights right into their eyes.

When I finished, he leaned forward. "What a pile of crazy. What's your next move? And remember that waiting for lab reports is not taking action."

"Darlene and I are going to shadow our suspects as well as we can by ourselves."

"Take some extra deputies if you need them. I'll authorize the overtime," he said, then added, "within limits."

"We'll conduct searches on our gold diggers. If they don't give us permission, we shouldn't have too much trouble coming up with probable cause. And we'll try to get the remaining family members to give us permission to conduct searches of their premises. We're already searching Joe's house again and the area around it for anything that might have been used as the primary weapon. And we'll conduct interviews with anyone that might have information about our gold hunters or the family."

Dad seemed satisfied with our planned approach. "You have to hate cases where you have too many suspects, but not one that's really good," he grumbled.

CHAPTER TWENTY-ONE

On Friday I got a call from Marge that the viewing was going to be held Saturday evening and that the triple funeral would be on Sunday afternoon. Sunday was an unusual day for a funeral—Saturdays or weekdays were the norm—but this was an unusual situation.

"I'm just doing the best I can," Marge said at one point in the conversation. I wondered how much help Jane and Andrew were being. Not much, I guessed.

Darlene and I went down one rabbit hole after another following leads. All of them petered out in the end. I hated to admit it, and I'd never tell Dad, but the truth was we *were* just waiting for the lab reports and hoping to fall onto a promising lead. We did keep tabs on our seven prime suspects. I let Darlene in on the fact that Eddie was my informant and had proved useful in the past. She just gave me a skeptical look.

We decided we would both attend the viewing and the funeral. We wanted to keep an eye out in case someone showed up we hadn't accounted for. We couldn't close the door on the possibility that someone we hadn't even considered was our killer. And we also wanted to watch our current batch of suspects closely. If one of them showed up and was acting strangely, we wanted to be there. Funerals were often an opportunity to see suspects interacting in an emotionally charged atmosphere.

Shantel took her intern out to Joe's house. They collected half a dozen objects that could have been the primary murder weapon, including a surprisingly clean golf club found in a gardening shed.

At three o'clock, Shantel finally got a report back from the lab. The skin found on the concrete alligator had come back as a match for Hank Junior. I called Darlene, who was at the main farm with Deputy Martel, searching vehicles and outbuildings for possible weapons.

"Interesting and very suggestive. But not enough to be conclusive," Darlene said over the phone.

"In fact, it could be counterproductive. If we arrest someone else for the murder, a defense attorney is going to propose that Hank killed Joe and then committed suicide by drug overdose," I said.

"Happy thought," she said morosely.

By the end of the day, between the search of Joe's house and farm, we had dozens of items for our crime scene techs to check for trace evidence. Darlene and Martel had been very selective. On such a large farm, there were literally thousands of tools that could have fit the descriptions that Dr. Darzi and the blood splatter expert gave us. Darlene chose to take only the most suggestive—ones that looked too clean or seemed to have been hidden.

We still needed to search Marge's, Clive's, Jane's and Andrew's vehicles, but we didn't have probable cause, which meant that they could just refuse to let us. I decided to wait until after the funeral to approach them, hoping they might be in a more receptive, less emotional state of mind.

Saturday dawned as a gorgeous spring day. The sun was a little warmer and the trees were beginning to show some of their bright green foliage. I got up, dressed, fed Ivy and headed for the Springtime in the Square celebration.

The festival activities took place in the town square around the courthouse, with all of the local churches and charities participating. When I got there at nine, everyone was setting up their booths. Dad had a small one where he and a couple of friends handed out election brochures, while Mauser drew the usual adoring crowd. But Chief Maxwell had his family, including a couple of impossibly cute grandchildren, passing out candy and bumper stickers at another booth on the other side of the square. Dad was going to have his work cut out for him this election.

I found the animal adoption booth sandwiched between the First Baptist Church and the Red Cross booths. I helped Cara and a few other volunteers carry and set up dog crates and cat cages before taking the leash of a rather hyper puppy that looked to be a mix of Dachshund and German Shepard. He was equal parts ugly and adorable.

The day spent in the sunshine helping Cara and the humane society would have been perfect if almost everyone who stopped by hadn't kept trying to ferret out information on the Parrish killings. The fact that I had the viewing that evening also prevented me from banishing the murders to the back of my mind. At least I scored brownie points with Cara for helping out.

After lending a hand with the teardown, I headed home to get a shower and dressed for the viewing. Digging in my closet, I hauled out my funeral clothes—a black jacket, pants and tie. I debated my gun and badge options before deciding on the more discreet shoulder holster and placing my badge in my inside coat pocket rather than hanging it on my belt. Emotions run high at funerals, but I didn't really expect to have to arrest anyone.

Cara had offered to come with me, but she hadn't known any of the Parrishes and I'd be stuck there from beginning to end. Besides, I needed to keep my eyes on everyone coming and going.

Marshall's Funeral Home was made up of two main

buildings. The original building was a large Victorian house built in the late 1890s. John Marshall was the first mortician in the family and he had bought the house in 1934. He'd been a carpenter who kept his money in a mattress instead of a bank, so when the Great Depression hit he left with cash. He'd bought the house for pennies on the dollar when it was about to go into foreclosure. George had decided that death would be a better business than construction. Eighty-plus years later, his great-grandson was running the operation and, by all accounts, making a healthy profit.

In 1994 they had built a large brick building that housed a chapel and an impressive casket showroom. As small as Adams County was, there were people all over north Florida who had roots there and had plans to come back when they were ready to spend eternity underground or in a bronze urn.

The viewing was scheduled for the chapel since none of the rooms in the original house came close to accommodating the expected number of mourners and gawkers. The chapel had been designed so that there could be two services with a divider between them, or one large service. Tonight they were going to need all the room they could get.

I arrived half an hour before the viewing was scheduled to start. It was supposed to run between seven and nine. Marge, Clive, Jane and Andrew were already there. The three coffins sat atop draped biers next to a podium at the front of the chapel. Hank Senior's was in the middle. His was open while the two coffins on either side were tastefully closed with pictures of the sons on stands next to them.

Marge and Jane were positioning the hundreds of flower arrangements around the room. It looked like they were playing some bizarre game, as one would move a flower arrangement to one location and then the other woman would eventually come by and move it somewhere else. Neither seemed to notice that the other one was undoing her work. Clive and Andrew just stood apart from the women and each other, looking awkward and uncomfortable.

Everyone in the family looked up when I came in and then immediately ignored me, which was fine. I stood at the back of the room, trying to fade into the woodwork.

Darlene arrived and we decided that she would station herself outside in her car, keeping an eye out for anything odd going on outside. Who knew? Maybe the murderer would come to the viewing, but not be able to bring himself to enter the chapel. Yeah, we were grasping at straws.

By seven there was already a large crowd of people. I watched as old friends who hadn't seen each other in a while shook hands and talked about the triple tragedy before moving on to discuss whatever was going on in their lives. Viewings are very much a social event in the south. They are about showing respect for the deceased and showing everyone *else* that you are showing respect for the deceased.

Most everyone paid their respects to Hank Senior first, before finding whichever Parrish family members they knew best and telling them how sorry they were for their losses. They took another few minutes to talk to anyone else they knew before quietly leaving.

Pete and his wife, Sarah, came in about eight.

"I hate funerals," Pete said to me as his wife went up to talk with Marge. Pete looked uncomfortable crammed into a dark suit two sizes too small.

"Wearing uncomfortable clothes at an uncomfortable social event where half the people are on an emotional cliff. What's not to like?" I asked sarcastically.

"At least you're being paid to be here," he tossed back.

"True. But I also have the added pressure of trying to come up with something useful out of all of this." I waved at the crowd.

"Your murderer is probably here," Pete acknowledged. "But they aren't liable to confess in front of everyone."

"I know. Just crossing t's and dotting i's," I said.

"Cara called me about taking her to the range."

"Really?" Even though she'd said she was going to do it,

I was surprised that she had. Apparently she was really serious about becoming more proficient with a handgun.

"I think having your insane ex-girlfriend in town has made her nervous."

"Ha, me too," I said. "Hopefully we can clear up these murders and Marcy'll leave town again."

"What the hell is all this about her hunting for Nazi gold?" Pete asked.

I explained all the idiocy surrounding the treasure hunt to Pete's great amusement.

"You sure do lead an interesting life. All I have going is a bar fight that landed two guys in the hospital and a bar full of folks who didn't see anything. And a domestic dispute that turned into a Mike Tyson fight. The husband lost most of his ear while the wife suffered a serious concussion. You getting along better with Darl?" he asked.

"I think so. Who knows? Maybe I'll get to where I like her better than you."

"Hey, now. We have a beautiful bromance going on."

I tried to keep an eye on the crowd as we bantered back and forth until Sarah came back over and she and Pete were able to make their escape.

After they left, I looked at my watch to see that I had more than half an hour before I could even hope that the viewing would begin to wind down.

Dad came in toward the end to pay his respects. He was wearing his dress uniform with a black armband. When Marge saw him, she went straight over and they talked for a few minutes.

After he went up to the coffins and stood for a moment, he came back to me. "What did Marge want to talk to you about?" I asked.

"Hank served in Vietnam. I'd told her I'd arrange an honor guard. She was just checking on that. The National Guard is sending a detail."

"I'm sure she appreciates your help."

"I'm sure she'd appreciate knowing who's killing her

family," he said abruptly and then added, "I don't mean to give you hard time. This isn't an easy case."

Dad hung around for a few more minutes, talking with folks. I knew that he hated to feel as if he was taking advantage of a situation to play politics, but in a situation like this there was a very thin line between duty, loyalty to a friend and plain old country politics.

CHAPTER TWENTY-TWO

At last my watch said it was nine o'clock so I texted Darlene and told her that she could head home. The last of the mourners came and went. Jane was standing by the caskets, talking with Andrew, while Marge straightened things that didn't need straightening. I stayed at the back of the chapel next to the double oak doors as Fredrick Marshall, the current patriarch of the Marshall clan, went around locking some of the doors and turning off all but the main lights. Then he walked over to Marge, talked to her for just a moment and then went to close Hank Senior's casket. But at that moment the door beside me opened and Joel Patrick walked in.

Joel was dressed in an old black coat and pants that probably would have been rejected by Goodwill. I was so surprised at his appearance that I allowed him to get halfway down the aisle before jogging up to intercept him.

I saw motion by the caskets. Jane had pushed past Andrew and was also heading to intercept Joel, who was strolling toward the three coffins as though there was no one else in the room.

"Jane," Joel said in a sad voice, but loud enough for everyone in the room to hear. Jane was standing right in front of him now.

"What are you doing here?" she asked, trying to whisper but failing completely. The rest of the room had gone silent and they were the focus of everyone's attention.

"Paying my respects, of course," he said and tried to walk around her. As I was coming up behind him, I saw Mr. Marshall move in front of the caskets. Everyone in the room, including Clive, Marge and Andrew, moved toward Joel as if we were all pins being drawn to a magnet.

Apparently realizing that he couldn't get through everyone, he turned back to Jane. "I'm sorry for your father's passing. He and I had our differences, but… And Hank Junior, he was a good kid. I liked him. Worked with Joe all those years ago. Those months in the hay fields were the best time of my youth." Joel was rambling. Jane was speechless and everyone else seemed unsure what to do.

"I'm sure that you mean well by coming here, but the viewing is over," I said, coming up behind him. He hadn't seen me when he came in and now he swung around and gave me a cold look that quickly turned back into fake grief.

"I just want a second," he said.

"That is up to the family," I said firmly.

Joel, his eyes wide and innocent, looked from Jane to Marge. "Really, I just…"

He didn't get any further then that. The door of the chapel was slammed open again with a bang, causing all of us to turn and look. Strolling up the aisle like an avenging angel on crack was Marcy, aiming a pump shotgun at all of us.

Two instincts warred inside of me. First was the need to protect, to step between Marcy and the others. The second instinct was the more rational one that screamed at me to jump behind the nearest pew because that woman was crazy. The first one, backed by years of training, won out.

"Marcy, put down the gun," I said calmly and firmly, while keeping both of my hands down by my sides. I stood between her and everyone else, but didn't move toward her.

"Larry, get out of my way," Marcy said through gritted

teeth. Then she shouted, "Don't move!" I turned my head slightly to see that Andrew had started to sidle away from everyone else.

"Everyone stay where you are," I said. "Marcy isn't going to hurt anyone. Are you?"

She seemed to take a long time to consider her answer. "What are you doing here?" she asked, and I wasn't sure who she was directing the question to.

"She's been lying to us," was the answer from Joel. "I came to find out why."

"When were you going to tell me?" Marcy asked him. They were talking around the rest of us.

"Deputy, you need to put an end to this. Arrest these two," Jane said to me.

"He's not arresting me. At least not until I've done what I came here to do," Joel said.

I'd figured out that Marcy must have followed Joel here. I was really kicking myself for telling Darlene that she could go home.

"Tell him what you did," Marcy said.

"That was an accident…" Joel started.

"Not you, you idiot, her," Marcy said disdainfully, jerking her head toward Jane and waving the shotgun around indiscriminately. I knew from our earlier years together that she knew how to use a shotgun, not that the pump shotgun needed a genius-level IQ to operate. I tried to keep one eye on Marcy's trigger finger which, so far, was staying safely outside the trigger guard.

"I don't know what you are talking about," Jane stated flatly.

"Liar!" Marcy screamed, and I watched her finger move closer toward the trigger guard. But it stopped before it got there and went back to resting on the side of the gun.

I really hoped that Marcy wouldn't shoot anyone. But as a deputy and as someone who wanted to protect the lives of everyone in the room, I had to consider the option of trying to stop her with deadly force. I thought about my Glock resting in its holster under my arm and wished I had worn my belt holster. I wasn't as proficient drawing from a shoulder holster and I was still ten yards from her. If Marcy went to shoot, I'd need to make a difficult headshot.

Most people watch movies and TV and believe that all an officer has to do is shoot the bad guy and the fight is over, but that is far from the case. In order to stop someone from shooting more people, you have to make that very difficult headshot. The small triangle formed by the eyes and nose is the kill switch. Shoot him just about anywhere else and a bad guy still has options. The only reason most criminals stop when they've been shot is because they are frightened and want the other guy to stop shooting at them. But if they want to, even with several mortal wounds, they can fight on for minutes.

So my calculation as I stood there was whether I could draw and fire a round from a holster I hadn't practiced with, and hit an area the size of a notecard on a possibly moving target, before she could shoot me. I doubted it. Shooting would have to be my last recourse.

"Marcy, listen to me. We can talk this out," I said, trying to keep a calm and reasoned tone.

"You bitch," she said to Jane, completely ignoring me. Marcy reached into her jeans pocket and took out an envelope, tossing it in Jane's direction. Envelopes don't fly very well, so it went only about ten feet before falling to the floor in the middle of the aisle. It landed face up, and I took my eyes off of Marcy just long enough to see that it had gone through the mail.

"What is that?" I asked, as much to get Marcy's angry eyes focused off of Jane as to find out what was in the letter.

"The truth that that lying, scheming bitch screwed us over!" Marcy yelled, but I took it as progress that she actually heard my question and answered me.

"How did she screw you?" I asked.

Marcy hesitated. She obviously wanted the truth to come out and I hoped she wanted that more than she wanted to throw Jane's guts all over the chapel.

"What did she do?" I prodded.

"Go ahead and look at it." She waved the shotgun from me to the letter.

Cautiously I moved forward, wondering if I should take the opportunity of being within ten feet of Marcy to rush her. If I got inside the swing of the barrel of the shotgun, I could control it enough to ensure that she couldn't point it at anyone while I wrestled it away from her. But no sooner had that thought occurred to me then she started to move back, keeping the distance between us at a range that would make it impossible for me to cross it before she was able to fire a load of birdshot, buckshot or a slug into me.

I settled for picking up the envelope. Everyone was watching me. I looked at the front. The letter was addressed to Marcy at her parents' address. There was no return address and the postmark was Monday. Jane was nervous, shifting from one foot to the other as I opened the envelope and took out a piece of paper.

I don't know what I expected to find, maybe a handwritten letter, but what I pulled out was a screen capture of the confirmation of a winning bid on eBay. The auction was for a gold-plated two-mark silver coin. The picture showed a Nazi eagle holding a wreath that encircled a swastika. The winning bid was by queenb222.

I turned to Jane and held the paper up to her. "Queenb222, I presume," I said.

Jane's face morphed into an excellent copy of the Wicked Witch of West's face as she went after Dorothy and her little dog too. "She's out of her mind," Jane growled, and I saw Andrew move away from Jane. The look on his face was clear evidence that he had absolutely no idea what Jane had been up to.

I turned back to Marcy. "So she bought a fake gold coin. Well, a real Nazi coin that had been gold-plated. What did she do with it?"

"She told us that it was part of the treasure. She said that she knew how we could find all of it."

"She told *you* this?"

"She told Hank and he told us." Marcy didn't like explaining things and I could tell that her patience was wearing thin.

"I'm just trying to understand all of this."

"He knew it wasn't real!" Jane yelled. I thought, *You are going to get yourself killed if you don't shut up.* "He was more than happy to use it to trick you into helping him hunt for his stupid gold."

"No, he believed you! But then he found out you lied to him and that's why he sent me this," Marcy screamed back and rattled the shotgun at Jane. "He wanted me to know that you were behind all this."

"Jane killed Hank Senior?" I asked, with the twofold purpose of getting information while staving off the moment when that shotgun got used.

"No, *he* did that," Marcy said and, to my surprise, pointed at Joel, whose mouth fell open while his head swiveled from side to side, looking for allies or enemies.

"No, I didn't," he finally managed in a very unconvincing performance.

"You shot him with Hank's crossbow. Hank told me."

"It was an accident," Joel shot back. "I told you, it was a freaking accident! Who even knew you could kill someone with one of those medieval contraptions?" he said and I was reminded of the fact that he was a city boy at heart.

"I pointed it at him and the damn thing just went off," Joel continued, using the classic "inanimate object did the killing" defense. Suddenly he stopped and looked at all of us, realizing that he'd just confessed to killing someone. "I really didn't mean to hurt him. I swear! I was there and Hank had told me to keep a lookout. He gave me that stupid crossbow. He even loaded it. I wouldn't have known how. I was walking around when I heard a tractor. I went to look, and I guess the old man had seen or heard something. I pointed the crossbow at him and told him to stop, but... I... Before

I knew it, the thing had gone off." He deflated like a bouncy house when the power is turned off and stumbled, reaching out to catch himself on the back of a pew.

"What did you do after that?" I asked Joel.

"I ran and told Hank that someone was coming, and we rushed back and tried to load the backhoe. But that got screwed up so we unhitched the truck and drove off."

"You took a shot at me by my gate."

"I wanted the book. We needed to find the gold to make it all worth it. I wouldn't have shot you," he said, but since he hadn't intended to shoot Hank Senior either, that wasn't much comfort to me.

"So who killed Joe?" I asked to the crowd at large.

"She did," Marcy said, pointing at Jane again with the gun. Jane was shaking her head and staring daggers at Marcy.

"How do you know that?" I asked Marcy.

"You're the detective, look in the damn envelope," she said. Sure enough, I hadn't noticed the small handwritten note left inside when I took out the eBay confirmation. I opened it now and read aloud: "The lead pipe she used is in the well. I'm so sorry. I had to protect her." The note was signed by Hank Junior.

"I didn't kill him," Jane said as though she was giving the opening remarks at her trial. "I hit him, but Hank was the one who crushed his head in with that alligator." The calmer her voice became, the more unhinged she sounded.

"Hank Junior loved Jane. He told me once that she was the only one in his family that understood him. She used that. She never really gave a damn about him," Marcy said with such venom that I realized she had actually cared about Hank Junior. *What a sad, toxic pair*, I thought.

"Marcy, I understand your anger," I said and began to ease down the aisle toward her, always aware that her mercurial personality could change in an instant. "You have every right to be mad. I swear to you that I'll help you," I said it and meant it. There are two types of people that are easily manipulated—those that have very weak personalities like Hank Junior and those who are volcanos of emotion like Marcy, and Jane had taken advantage of both of them. In the end, Hank killed himself with drugs and Marcy exploded. I felt sorry for both of them.

When I was about six feet from Marcy, her instinct for freedom kicked in and she turned and ran. I lunged for her, but missed. Regaining my footing, I started after her, but the door opened and Darlene was standing there. Marcy couldn't stop and Darlene, in one continuous move, took the shotgun from Marcy, threw it aside and grabbed Marcy into a bear hug.

"What's going on?" she asked, holding onto the struggling Marcy. I turned to see Joel suddenly come to his senses and leap at Jane.

"Hold her," I said to Darlene. "Stop!" I yelled at Joel and Jane. "You two break it up," I said, trotting over to where Joel was trying to strangle Jane as she attempted to claw his eyes out.

Clive, who'd been standing quietly with his eyes wide open throughout the whole ordeal, seemed to wake up and headed toward the two rolling on the ground. I saw what was going to happen and cringed, unable to stop it. Joel and Jane tumbled into the bier that Joe's coffin was resting on. It teetered and I thought for a second, as I grabbed ahold of Joel, that it might stay upright. But as Clive reached for Jane, she jerked away, hitting one of the legs of the bier again.

Seemingly in slow motion, the casket tipped over and fell to the floor. The lid opened and the headless body of Joe Parrish rolled across the floor and came to rest against the podium. I heard a cry of anguish from poor Marge just before she fell to her knees, crying, and a shout of "Oh, no!" from Mr. Marshall, who almost ran over the top of us trying to catch the body.

Clive managed to get the upper hand on Jane. With me pulling Joel back and Clive tugging on Jane, we managed to get them apart. I didn't have any handcuffs, but of course Darlene did. She got Marcy cuffed then came over and helped me cuff Joel and Jane, then I called dispatch and asked them to send backup. As I hung up, I noticed I had several missed calls from Darlene, since I'd turned my phone off once the viewing started.

Once Marcy, Jane and Joel were all in handcuffs, I took Darlene aside.

"The deputy we had keeping an eye on Marcy called and said that he'd had to answer a call and, when he was coming back, Marcy's car passed him going the other direction. By the time he got turned around, she was out of sight. I tried to call you, but after the third try I thought I ought to come back and see what was going on," Darlene explained.

"Thanks," I said sincerely.

Darlene and I talked to Marcy while we were waiting for backup. She had just found the letter that night. It had been tossed in with her parents' mail, and her mom had been too wrapped up in taking care of her dad to notice.

Marcy seemed genuinely shocked that we were going to charge her with a laundry list of offenses. She became a lot more cooperative when I said that the State Attorney would probably be willing to waive some of the more serious charges like assault with a deadly weapon and kidnapping for her cooperation in prosecuting Joel and Jane.

"But I didn't kidnap anyone!" she argued. I had to point out that the law defined the confining of someone in a controlled space as kidnapping. Holding us all at gunpoint in the chapel more than qualified.

I felt a little sorry for her so I agreed to hook her up with a halfway decent attorney that would work for cheap.

We watched as Mr. Marshall tried to calm Marge and convince her that they could go ahead with the funeral the next day if she was up to it. Clive had helped Marshall put Joe back inside the coffin. When I asked Marshall why the lid came open, he said that it was their practice to leave the lids unlocked until the funeral in case a member of the family wanted to place something in the casket with the body.

"We'll be reviewing the policy," Mr. Marshall said in his

most solemn voice.

Dad had heard about the ruckus at the funeral home on his radio and came by to get the details.

"Crazy people. But why did Jane set all this in motion?" he asked. I knew that the criminals that bothered him the most were the ones that were just evil for no reason.

"What I got out of her after we had her in cuffs was that she started it just to screw with Hank Junior, who seemed to be getting back in his father's good graces. Then, when her dad was killed, she saw it as an opportunity to cash out the farm. She knew that Joe wanted out of the farm in order to invest in a machine shop. So she was all excited that they'd be getting a cash windfall that could be used to clear up some of her debts, but when she went to talk to him about it, she learned that he'd had a change of heart and wanted to fight for the farm to honor their father. She got so mad that she hit him with a lead pipe that was lying in the garage. Then she didn't know what to do so she called Hank and begged him to help her. His solution was to crush Joe's skull and get rid of the pipe, hoping that we wouldn't be able to come up with a murder weapon or a motive. Without those, he figured it would be hard to prosecute anyone."

"You told me he left his DNA on the statue."

"He wasn't thinking very clearly, but it still would have been a hard case to prove."

Darlene walked up. "But he found out that she'd faked the gold coin thing and that pushed him over the edge," she filled in.

"Exactly," I said. "Hank must have searched Jane's computer, found the eBay receipt and realized that his beloved sister had been cruelly playing with his mind."

"Evil," Dad said.

"Pretty much," I agreed. "So he sent that note to Marcy, probably because he was really an okay guy and felt bad for getting her involved in everything. Then he took the pipe from wherever he'd stashed it after the murder, threw it down the well, then took a bunch of happy drugs and went off to die in the woods," I summed up the sad tale.

Dad congratulated us both on finally closing the case, and I thanked Darlene again for coming to my rescue. We agreed that we'd meet at the office on Sunday to begin the long process of writing reports and organizing everything for the prosecution.

When I finally got home, I almost tripped over a large cardboard box in the living room. There was a note on it that said: *I hope you don't mind. I've been spending so much time over here that I thought I'd bring a few of my things.* The box contained some clothes, shoes, a few books and an assortment of other personal items. *Doesn't mean anything,* I thought, smiling in spite of myself.

I found Cara curled up in bed with Alvin and Ivy asleep beside her. I undressed and slipped in quietly next to her, trying hard not to disturb them. It felt good to be between the covers, even though I knew I'd be dreaming of crazy women with shotguns and headless corpses. I sighed contentedly, thinking how winter would officially be over in just a couple of days. I was looking forward to a quiet spring.

Larry Macklin returns in:

April's Desires
A Larry Macklin Mystery–Book 6

Here's a preview:

I was on call Sunday when dispatch sent me out to the crime scene that would ruin my day. A body had been found in the backyard of a house in one of the older and seedier parts of Calhoun.

It was a beautiful morning, pleasantly warm with just a hint of the summer heat to come. April is one of the best months in north Florida. I tried not to think about the gruesome scene that was waiting for me and rolled down the window, enjoying the moment.

Though I didn't know it yet, this would be far from an ordinary case—no drug deal gone bad, suicide, accident or overdose. Death is never good, but some cases are resolved quickly, easily and with a hefty dose of justice. Other investigations try the foundations of our system. This was going to be one of the latter.

The small wood-frame house was rundown, its yard more dirt than grass. A couple of older cars were parked haphazardly in the driveway and two Adams County Sheriff's patrol cars were lined up at the curb. I pulled in behind them. As I got out of my car, one of the deputies, a woman who'd joined the department a year before, came up to meet me.

"Hey, Sandy, what have we got?"

"Somebody went to town on this kid," she said, obviously shaken up by the scene.

I'd worked with Matti Sanderson a few times. She was tough and professional. Her solid 5'9" frame always looked comfortable wearing her uniform and equipment. Unlike some rookies, Sandy seemed a natural, so if she was shaken up then it must have been bad.

"Martel is watching over the body. We've got three people in the house. One of them, David Benson, called it in. I've been out here making sure that they don't leave and that no one else tries to enter. I hope you don't mind, but I went ahead and told dispatch that you're going to need the crime scene techs."

"Good job. Run some crime scene tape across the driveway and get someone else out here to help. If none of our deputies are available, see if you can get a trooper from the highway patrol or an officer from the Calhoun police." On Sunday mornings we usually ran a light detail. If there was an accident or another emergency, then we had to take help from wherever we could find it.

"When someone shows up, go inside and make sure that the witnesses are behaving. Keep them separate."

It was probably too late to keep them from talking to each other, but it was better to close the barn door after the cows were out than to never close the door at all. Or whatever.

I retrieved a pair of rubber gloves from the trunk of my car, put on protective booties and headed around to the back of the house. The side of the house was almost completely hidden by azaleas that hadn't been trimmed in a decade or more. I had to step around an old screen that had fallen from one of the windows, but I knew it wasn't a clue as it was half buried by leaves and dirt.

Deputy Andy Martel was standing near the screened-in back porch, looking at anything except the body of the young man that lay about ten feet from the steps of the porch. He was on his side in a fetal position, his hands raised as though to protect his head from the blows that had crushed his skull. I understood what had bothered Sandy. He looked like a child curled up, defenseless against the onslaught that had killed him.

"Have you found anything interesting?" I asked Martel.

"Nope."

He was the most laconic deputy I'd ever met. Most cops love to hear themselves talk, but not Martel. If you wanted information from him, you had to ask. Someone had told me it was because Martel's family was from northern Wisconsin. Something about those long winters, I guess.

"Do we have a name?"

"Todd Harper."

Todd? Something about the name and the body rang a bell. I bent down and gently lifted the elbow that was blocking most of his face, then backed away quickly, feeling dizzy. My mind froze as I tried to make sense of what I was seeing. Then it raced ahead, considering all the possible ramifications of this murder.

Of course the name had rung a bell. I had seen the young man just the afternoon before. I couldn't prevent my mind from replaying the events of Saturday.

I'd spent the morning in Tallahassee with my girlfriend, Cara Laursen. We'd strolled through the arts and crafts at the Downtown Marketplace in the city's chain of parks, then sat on the terrace at Harry's and enjoyed some of the best New Orleans-style food this side of the Crescent City. We were headed home when I remembered that Pete Henley, my old partner, had wanted me to come to his daughter's softball game that afternoon. Eager to keep the beautiful day going, I looked over at Cara.

"Would you like to go to a softball game?"

She gave me a funny look. "I didn't know that you were a fan."

"It's Pete's daughter. She's got a big game this afternoon. Scouts coming and the whole bit."

"She a senior?"

"No, junior, but with a good game Pete says she might be able to lock up a scholarship. She's been contacted by a couple of schools already. And they're playing Leon High

School today."

"She must be excited."

"I'm not sure who's more excited, her or Pete. With two daughters and the hope that they'll both go to college in the next few years, he's desperate for some financial help. Deputies don't exactly pull in the big bucks." I certainly knew that to be true. Even without kids, there were months that I felt like I had to scrape up the money for my bills.

"I'm game. Pun intended," Cara said, flashing a smile.

"You play any sports?" I asked naively.

"Are you kidding? You've met my parents. They both think that team sports are the stepping stones to conformity, which leads to the subjugation of the soul," she answered with a grin.

I should have known better. Cara's mom and dad were what I'd imagine you'd get if you dropped an Irish country girl and a Viking warrior down in the middle of a commune. In fact, they currently lived in a co-op down in Gainesville that was only a few steps removed from a commune.

We parked in the Adams County High School lot, where several cars and a couple of buses were taking up about half the spaces. We walked out to the softball field where dozens of people were milling about while another seventy-five people sat in the bleachers, watching the Leon High girls warming up on the field.

I saw Pete right away. At almost three hundred pounds, he was hard to miss. He was standing near the dugout, talking to his oldest daughter, Jenny, who was dressed in her uniform and trying not to look like she was talking to her dad. I spotted Pete's younger daughter, Kim, sitting in the stands with her mom, Sarah.

We walked over to Pete and Jenny, whose eyes lit up as soon as she caught sight of me. I figured that she had been standing there looking for a way to escape her dad, and I was her salvation.

"Mr. Macklin. Wow! It's so cool you came," she said, interrupting her father and causing him to look around.

"Hey, Larry!" the big guy said, all smiles. "Cara, how are you?" he asked, pulling her into a big bear hug. He had recently given her a few shooting lessons out at the department's gun range and they had quickly formed a mutual admiration society.

"I was just telling Jenny to listen to Coach Terry. He's been after her all season to—"

"I've got it, Dad. Don't worry."

"And don't get nervous."

"You're the one that's nervous."

"I'm the one that's going to have to shell out the big bucks for college if you don't get a scholarship," he joked. Pete had one of the best relationships with his family of any deputy in the department. Even though my father was the sheriff, Pete was my model for how to do the job and have a home life that made the job worth doing.

"I've got this," Jenny said.

"She's the starting pitcher today," Pete said proudly.

Jenny blushed and rolled her eyes.

"I've got to go warm up."

"Hug for luck," Pete said, giving her a quick one before she turned and trotted through the gate onto the field.

We all went up into the stands to sit with Sarah and Kim. Sarah was one of the nicest people I'd ever met, with a dry sense of humor and eyes that were soft but deep. She reminded me of the folks that my grandmother had called "old souls." Granny would always say that they were too wise to have only lived once.

I found myself sitting between Kim and Cara. "Are you working on any murders?" Kim asked me.

She was fourteen and, to her father's blushing admiration, wanted to go into law enforcement. The young lady had come out just a month earlier to help with a search for a missing person, and her observation of a group of vultures had led to the body being discovered inside a drainage pipe.

"Not right now. And I'm happy about that," I told her,

smiling.

"Yeah, I can understand that."

"How are you doing?" I was worried that finding a dead body might have caused her some distress, but I avoided mentioning it directly in case I dredged up memories that she was trying to push down.

"Okay," she answered, then went on as though she had read between the lines of my question. "I had some nightmares after finding that body. But they're gone now."

"So have you changed your mind about being a cop?"

"No. When I told Mom about the bad dreams, she said that my imagination was probably worse than the reality."

Pete had kept her back so that she hadn't actually seen the bloated and decaying body inside the culvert, but having seen it myself I doubted that her mother was right.

"So she bought me a book called *Death's Acre* about the body farm they have up in Tennessee."

My eyebrows lifted.

Pete was sitting on the other side of Kim and had been listening in on our conversation. "I'm not sure you should be telling the whole world that we got you that book," he told her.

"You didn't want to," she said accusingly.

"Mother knows best, I guess," he responded.

"I don't have nightmares anymore," Kim the realist told him. "And I may want to be a pathologist." She turned back to me. "Did you know that, after the first twelve hours, insects and the different stages that they go through are the best way to tell when someone died?"

"I'm afraid that I did," I joked with her. Actually, it wasn't that much of a joke. I really did wish that I knew less about dead bodies and their decomposition.

"I think it's really interesting. Now I wish I could have seen that body," Kim said as much to her dad as to me.

"No, you don't," Pete said firmly. "When you become a pathologist you can look at all the corpses you want, but for right now you should be thinking about kid stuff."

"You take me out to the range," she responded. I'd seen her shoot and she wasn't bad.

"Hush," Pete said, looking around comically. "You're going to get your mother and me thrown in the poky for child abuse."

I noticed that several of the other folks sitting around us were trying to suppress smiles. Probably everyone in the stands knew Pete and his family.

Out on the field, practice was over. The two teams came out and lined up in front of their dugouts, and we all stood for the national anthem.

"Crap," I heard Pete mutter under his breath just after we sat back down. I looked over and saw him staring at a young man who'd just walked up to the fence next to the home team's dugout. Pete was shooting daggers at the back of the kid, who looked scruffy even from this distance.

The game went well for Jenny. She didn't allow any runs and only a few hits during the first seven innings. Whenever she returned to the dugout she would give the young man a slight wave and a quick look, but at one point I thought I also saw a frown cross her face. Several times I heard Pete actually growl, and Sarah would place her hand on his knee, restraining him as effectively as if she had wrapped both hands around him.

Jenny was finally taken out of the game and a relief pitcher put in. Adams County ended up losing, but it was clearly not because of Jenny's performance. With the game over, we all made our way down the bleachers. I could feel the stands rock with each step that Pete took. He was watching the young man, who was heading directly for the team as they came off of the field.

Jenny stopped outside the gate and said something to the young man, who put his hand on her arm. She backed away from him, and he immediately stepped toward her again.

I was following Pete with Cara, Sarah and Kim trailing us. Pete was focused on Jenny and the man and I decided to stick close to him. This had the feel of a situation that could spiral out of control quickly.

The man put his hand on Jenny's arm again and this time she slapped it away. When that happened, Pete broke into a jog and I ran to catch him. Jenny saw her father coming and stepped between him and the young man.

"No!" she shouted. Behind Jenny, I saw a slight smile cross the man's lips.

"Get your hands off of her!" Pete said through clenched teeth as he continued to bull his way forward. At this point I managed to cut in front of him with only six feet to go before he'd be nose to nose with them. Pete pushed me another three feet as I tried to slow his momentum.

"Pete, cool down," I said, planting my feet and putting my hands against his chest.

"Get out of my way," he said, looking past me at the young man.

"Todd's leaving," Jenny said to Pete.

"He'd better be running," Pete said louder than was necessary. A small crowd of people was now watching our little tableau. I even saw a couple of phones pointed our way.

"Stop it!" I barked straight into Pete's face and, for the first time since this had started, I had his full attention.

"He grabbed her arm," he growled at me.

I had never seen Pete go full Papa Bear. His anger was truly impressive. I decided that I needed to focus a bit on the other half of the problem. "You need to get the hell out of here," I told Todd, who had only three feet, Jenny and me between him and an unpleasant evening at the hospital.

"No way. This is a public—" he started, but Jenny turned to him and put a stop to his suicidal declaration.

"Go home, Todd. I told you I don't want you here," she said, clearly frustrated with him.

"I want to see you again."

"Not now."

"Meet me later," he pleaded.

"Can't you understand, she doesn't want to see you," Pete said and started pushing forward again like a bulldozer.

"Maybe," Jenny said to Todd, clearly not wanting to, but eager to bring an end to this embarrassing situation.

"When?" Todd asked.

Pete growled.

"Later. Just go!"

"My house." And then he reached out, possessively running his hand up Jenny's waist toward her breast.

A batboy chose just that moment to stop within arm's reach of us with a duffle bag full of bats and Pete, quick as lightning, reached out and grabbed one of the bats. I saw it happen in that weird slow motion of accidents and made my decision. I lowered my hold on Pete and then pushed forward, taking him down using leverage. I had to clench my teeth and lock my arms around his legs to keep him from struggling free.

"I'll take care of you. Don't you come near my family again, you son of a bitch!" Pete raged. I heard the bat thump on the ground a couple of times as I clung on for dear life.

Anyone watching at that moment or seeing the video later would have thought that Pete was completely out of control. I knew differently. The man had a .45 caliber Glock 21 on his waist that he could have pulled at any time. He was the department's firearms instructor and was one of the fastest and best shots I'd ever met. Pete never made a move toward his gun. But that argument paled next to the frothing anger that everyone could see.

Holding onto Pete, I couldn't tell what was going on behind me, but Cara told me later that Todd took off as soon as Pete grabbed the bat. Jenny had looked mortified, and Sarah had taken her to their car as Pete tried to regain a measure of his composure—no small challenge with me wrapped around his legs.

"He's gone. You can let go of me," Pete said in a small voice. I turned my head to see the crowd beginning to disperse. Half of the audience looked embarrassed while the other half looked like they had enjoyed the show.

I helped Pete to his feet. The batboy was still standing

there in shock. Pete, shamefaced, gave him back the bat. Two large men, one of whom I recognized as the coach, were standing behind us.

"Pete, I've got to report this," the coach said.

"Mr. Henley, I should tell you that I don't know if I can let you back on school property. We have very strict rules about fighting at school events," said the other man, who I later learned was the principal. "Especially adults."

"I'm sorry," Pete said lamely. "I'm…" He wanted to explain, but he had been on the other side too many times and knew that you can't explain your way out of a justified punishment. He just put up his hands and said, "You're right," then turned and started toward his car.

"Pete," I said, catching up with him. "Don't worry. I'll talk to Dad."

Pete and I both knew that videos were going to be circulated and that this was going to be a problem for the department. I would've never used the fact that my father was the sheriff for my own benefit—truth was, I probably couldn't—but I was more than willing to do anything I could to help Pete. If I had any influence with Dad, I'd use every bit of it to defend a man I knew to be one of our best.

"This is going to be a shit storm," Pete said morosely. "I saw the cameras."

"Maybe no one will post the video," I said, knowing that it was probably uploading to various platforms as we spoke.

"I hate that kid. Jenny tried to break it off with him a month ago, but he won't let go. Scares me." Pete stopped and looked me in the eye. "How many cases of assault, stalking, even murder, have started like this?" he asked.

"You aren't wrong. But you've put yourself in a position now where you can't go anywhere near him. Look, I'll help you with this any way I can. Right now, you need to go home and take care of Jenny. Don't worry about anything except making things right at home." I knew that a plea to his nesting instinct was the best way to get him focused on something productive.

"You're right." Pete looked toward his car where his wife and two daughters were talking. Jenny looked devastated as her mother comforted her.

After we left the school, I called Dad, explaining what had happened and warning him that there were going to be some PR issues over the incident. He thanked me for the heads-up while cursing social media.

ACKNOWLEDGMENTS

Thanks to Liane Schrader for being an excellent beta reader and cheerleader for the series. And a big thank you to everyone who has read this series so far—I am humbled by how well it has done and I'm glad that others seem to enjoy reading this series as much as I enjoy writing it.

As always, I have to recognize the amazing and constant support and encouragement I've received from H. Y. Hanna, as well as her original cover design. Words cannot express my appreciation for all her help.

If you can have one thing in life, choose luck. I was very lucky indeed to have met a woman who could be my friend, my editor and my wife. Much of what I've accomplished, including this series, could not have been done without Melanie.

Original Cover Concept by H. Y. Hanna
Cover Design by Robin Ludwig Design Inc.
www.gobookcoverdesign.com

ABOUT THE AUTHOR

A. E. Howe lives and writes on a farm in the wilds of north Florida with his wife, horses and more cats than he can count. He received a degree in English Education from the University of Georgia and is a produced screenwriter and playwright. His first published book was *Broken State*; the Larry Macklin Mysteries is his first series and he has plans for more. Howe is also the co-host of the "Guns of Hollywood" podcast, part of the Firearms Radio Network. When not writing or podcasting, Howe enjoys riding, competitive shooting and working on the farm.